Also By Bob Freeman

CAIRNWOOD MANOR SERIES
Shadows Over Somerset
Keepers of the Dead

TALES OF THE LIBER MONSTRORUM
First Born

Also By Greg Mitchell

THE COMING EVIL TRILOGY
The Strange Man
Enemies of the Cross
Dark Hour

Rift Jump
Rift Jump, Vol. 2: Sara's Song

Infernal City

HITMEN: Four Tales of Magick, Monsters, and Murder

HALLOWEEN HOUSE

BOB FREEMAN and GREG MITCHELL

GENRE
EXPERIENCE

Hallowe'en House
Copyright 2018 Bob Freeman and Greg Mitchell
ISBN: 9781726636674

Published by Genre Experience

Cover and interior art by Bob Freeman
Artwork Copyright 2018 Bob Freeman

Introduction

WHAT'S IN A NAME?

Like arguably every fan of science fiction and horror, as a kid I wanted to escape to fantastic, imaginary worlds, battle monsters, win the girl, and go on epic quests with my favorite heroes. Simply reading about those adventures, however, never quite satisfied me. No, I wanted to literally transpose myself *into* those stories, to such an extent that I drew pictures of myself in action poses, cut them out, and taped them inside my favorite comics (now you newfangled kids just use Photoshop).

As a middle-schooler, when the first inklings of my passion for writing began to bloom, I typically wrote myself as the main character—using my name, my friends' names, pulling from my immediate life experiences. It was all pretty shallow, I can safely admit as an adult, but for one brief moment I would read over what I wrote and feel like a real hero. I remember once discovering an ad in the back of a magazine for a small press that, for about twenty-five bucks, would take your name and basic personal description (brown hair, blue eyes), and place you in the middle of a generic plot that allowed you to "star in your own story." Man, I jumped at that, and it was such a thrill to see my name in there and read of my fictional exploits.

As I grew up, well, not a whole lot changed. I *still* have managed to fenagle my way into other's stories. It still gives me a little thrill, though admittedly not the same rush of wish fulfillment as it once did when I was a kid. But I suppose it's that strange desire to see myself fictionalized that has led to the book you now hold in your hands.

I "met" Bob Freeman some years back. We both contributed weird horror stories to an anthology (no, I wasn't the main character), and I was immediately taken in by his work. The story he submitted was "Queen's Gambit". It read just like a great Dan Curtis TV horror special from the '70s and even reminded me of *The Exorcist III*. So I wrote Bob to tell him how much I liked it, and we soon "friended" each other on Facebook, and that was that.

Only one day Bob made mention on Facebook that he was cooking up a new tale of terror and asked, "Hey, who wants to get namedropped in this thing?"

Well... You know me.

I pounced on that post—"Me! Me! Me!" And my persistence, or the fact that Bob didn't have any other takers, won out. Bob wrote me into his next short story, "The Cabin In the Woods". Lest you think it was anything too terribly exciting, I don't actually appear in the story, at all, but rather my corpse does. And later my skinned, severed head. It's a thing.

Anyway, the fictional Greg Mitchell lived a life I had often dreamed about in real life—fighting all manner of supernatural evils while riding off into the sunset with the beautiful girl after the killin' was done. However, my namesake's fun had run its course when he met a grisly end, only to be avenged by the true star of all of Bob's work—Occult Detective Landon Connors.

After my single guest appearance, Bob and I continued our correspondence. I became a big fan of his work (not just because I'm in it), and once I discovered his artistic abilities, I even hired him to do the cover art for my own foray into the weird occult genre, *HITMEN: Four Tales of Magick, Monsters, and Murder*. As our working relationship, and later our friendship, grew, I still often thought back to the late, great monster hunter-no-more Greg Mitchell. Bob made mention of Mitchell in a few of his other tales—even going so far as to use my own likeness in depicting him!—and ideas began to form in my mind as to what kind of a life the character must have led. It wasn't very long before I thought "I want to write a story about Greg Mitchell".

Even for *my* ego (he says with tongue firmly planted in cheek), I thought that might be a little much, if not completely self-serving, so I didn't immediately propose the idea. But it just sounded like a lot of fun, humility be abolished. So, finally, in the summer of 2017, while vacationing with my wife over our fifteenth wedding anniversary, no less, I could hold my tongue no longer. I texted Bob and asked if he wanted to collaborate with me on a Greg Mitchell/Landon Connors team-up. We would each take turns writing chapters with no forethought and no planning. Every chapter would be a surprise to the other, and if it made any sort of sense at all, maybe we'd show it to people.

It started as simply as that, and that's just what we've done, and since you're about to dive in, provided I ever end this introduction, you can see that we thought it was worth putting it on public display. We hope you agree.

So, there you go. A story about the fictional Greg Mitchell, co-written by the real Greg Mitchell. Thanks to Bob for incorporating me into his fascinating mythology and giving me an opportunity put my own spin on my namesake.

-Greg Mitchell
(the real one)
September 13, 2018

Chapter One

WITH SILENT STEPS, he strode down the hospital corridor, eyes fixed intently ahead as he navigated the halls to his destination. An errant laugh caught his attention, and Greg Mitchell glanced to the nurses' station, where three portly women in scrubs gathered around a cell phone, cycling through social media, ogling cute cat memes while trading stories about their small children. Greg always found it funny in a not-so-funny way, how hospital staff could carry on in such trivial distractions while, all around them, men, women, and children were fighting to live. Waiting rooms were filled to the brim with worried and fearful family members, wondering if this would be the day their lives were forever scarred.

But no, really, keep playing on your phone, he thought, giving his head a mild shake.

In truth, Greg hated hospitals. They were anxious, uncertain places, and they always seemed to attract the very things he was hoping to avoid on this occasion. Even now, he felt eyes on him—and not from the staff or patients. Spirits lurked here, festering, oppressive forces that treated the suffering of a hospital room as Must-See TV. No doubt those infernal shapes crowded about, sharing a bowl of popcorn as they watched parents fretting over the fate of their small children, or spouses

preparing to leave behind the love of their lives. The last thing Greg needed right now was to draw their notice—or, worse, to have one such shade latch on to him and follow him home.

Best to keep a low profile. To see this business through and leave.

Doing his best to quell his own anxieties, which would surely draw those hellborn spirits like a magnet, Greg rounded the corner, spotting his sister pacing restlessly in front of a closed door.

She sighted him, as well, and paused. Frowned.

At her side was his mother, face red and wet with tears, blubbering into a balled-up tissue. The two women had been in some silent, urgent communication that he'd unwittingly interrupted, and he slowed as their attention fell on him. His mom let out a small cry, his presence one burden too many for her, and he reconsidered his visit.

Her anguished wail did not go unnoticed by her grandchildren, whom Greg saw seated in two nearby chairs. His niece and nephew— seven and nine, respectively—were glued to their tablets, tuned out to reality. But hearing their grandmother's warble shook them from their screen-induced stupor and they glanced to him, eyes widening in hesitant excitement.

"Uncle Greg!" his nephew cried and stood, as if to come hug him, but the lad's mother stayed his advance. Scowling at Greg, she addressed her children in a sugary voice, "Why don't you take a break and go with Gramma? I saw a snack machine back down the other hall. Okay?"

The boy pointed to his uncle. "But I wanted—"

"*Now*, Luke."

Luke gave one last, forlorn look to his uncle and collected his sister. The children moped off, Greg's mother sobbing anew as she led the kids from the building confrontation.

Greg took another couple steps forward, but his sister crossed the distance in a single stride, jabbing a finger in his direction, her face screwed up in hot rage. "What do you think you're doing here?" she demanded in a harsh, barely contained whisper. "I should call the cops, you know that?"

Greg pursed his lips, sighing through his nose. "Do whatever you feel you need to do," he gently told her.

"You think she needs this now? That *any* of us do?"

"He asked for me."

His sister's fury subsided, but only for a moment.

"This isn't easy for me, either, Kat," Greg added.

He waited a moment more, to see if she had any more fight, but Kathrine finally stood down, her head bowed, teeth on edge. He supposed that was as much approval as he was likely to get from his big sister.

Stepping around her, he angled on the room that waited—and entered.

There, on the bed, pale and weak, lay the echo of his father. Bro. Bill Mitchell had been a pillar of fire, leading the congregation of the First Baptist Church of Mountain Rest, Arkansas, like they were the children of Israel navigating the desert following the Exodus. He'd been a surety to so many, a towering fortress of ironclad will and determination, unshakeable in his convictions and demanding the same of any who would follow Christ alongside him.

Now, he was merely an old man, his red-blonde beard having grown scraggy and unmanaged, his wispy hair oily and uncombed. He'd lost weight since Greg had seen him last, and the sight was a shock. Was this the man he had feared for so long? The one who had expected nothing less than perfection? In his youth, Bro. Bill was an icon to rival Superman, but Greg now saw that, somewhere in the intervening years, he'd outgrown his father—in more ways than one.

He neared the aged man. The room was quiet, save the steady beeps of the machines that kept Bro. Bill alive, following his recent stroke. Everything in Greg told him to hate this man, and maybe there had been a time in his teenage years—at the height of their lifelong battle, before Greg had left home for a war of another kind—when he had. But now, looking at the frail, dying man before him, Greg only felt compassion for him.

"Dad," he said, breaking the silence, ready to get down to business.

He'd not spoken to his father in some years and thought this situation a terrible excuse to remedy that.

Bill Mitchell opened one dewy eye, glancing about the room in sudden fright, before settling on his only son. "Lad," he breathed in relief. "You made it."

"I really can't stay long," Greg said, mindful not only of the devils who prowled these halls looking for sensitive souls to torment, but also more *mundane* pursuers. His war did not come without its share of casualties, and the authorities would never truly comprehend the nightly battles waged by him and his fellow Outriders. To the evening news, Greg Mitchell was a not a hero protecting the world of man from the age of nightmares. Rather, he was a wanted fugitive. A thief and, yes, much to Kathrine's scorn, a murderer. He'd killed men. Evil men, to be sure. Cultists and those who had aligned themselves with dark, eldritch forces—and even then only when there was absolutely no other way to spare the world from slipping off the brink into unfathomable chaos. Still, crimes were crimes, and he knew he must keep a low profile.

Despite the difficulties his calling presented, there were many reasons why he'd taken up this cause of others, to protect the innocent—most notably because it was *right*. He supposed he owed that insatiable need to make things right to the dying man in the hospital bed. And for that reason, if for no other, he was here today.

Bill weakly patted the armrest on his bed, as if searching for his son's hand, but Greg made no move to meet it. He merely watched, his heart heavy, wishing there was more he could do to soothe the old preacher's passing.

"Needed to talk," the man gasped around the breathing tube in his throat. "You and I…we've needed to talk for a long time."

Greg furrowed his brow. "Yes, sir."

"I was so hard on you, growing up…"

Greg recalled the lashes he'd suffered, but knew things had not always been so severe. He remembered his father, though strict, used to laugh and play with him when he was a small boy. It was only later, when he got older…when his "gifts" began to manifest, that the son suddenly appeared as an enemy to his once-loving father. After that, Bro. Bill looked on him as the spawn of Satan, believing only harsher punishment would stem the growing tide of evil.

"You were," Greg acknowledged without judgment or approval, merely stating a fact.

Now the man wept, his broken voice a gasp. "I've a lot to answer for, when I meet the Lord…"

Greg softened, thinking of the blood on his own hands. *Am I a good man?* "Yes, sir. We both do."

"I only ever wanted to protect you, lad… I saw a dark road ahead of you, and I would've died to spare you that. I thought I could beat the devil out of you, but…but maybe I just drove you into his arms."

So, was this it, then? A death bed confessional, the reason for his summons?

"I don't ask you to forgive me," his father said. "Only to understand…"

"I understand," Greg told him, thankful he wasn't asked to forgive. Perhaps he did forgive him, in the way one forgives a neighbor's dog that barks, growls, and snaps at those passing by his fence. It was simply the nature of the beast. In that way, he did forgive his father, knowing the man had done his best.

Even if his best wasn't good enough.

"No." The old man grew sharper, clutching the railing and pulling himself nearer. "No, son, you *don't* understand. Not yet." Fidgeting in bed, Bro. Bill rummaged beneath his pillow, finally producing a crumpled slip of paper bearing the hospital's letterhead. On it, a single address, shakily scrawled in ball point pen. He thrust it out for his son to take, but Greg only stared at it.

"What is it?"

Waving it, the man sputtered, "Hell."

This caught the Outrider's attention.

Exhausted from his ordeal, the old man simply let the scrap fall to the bed, and Greg bent over to read the address.

"It's a *house*," his father elaborated, tired. "But it's not there all the time. Only on October 31st…and only once every thirty years…"

Greg frowned, curious, his eyes darting back to his pale father.

"You ever wonder why I was so scared of you, son?"

Greg shook his head.

Bill grinned, but it was a sad expression. "Because I saw myself in you… I recognized all the signs. I knew you were sensitive… Didn't *see* things the way most people do… I know because I was like you, too. Once."

"*What?*"

The man relaxed in his bed with a groan, shutting his eyes tight, looking miserable. "I ran from it. Ignored it. Pretended I didn't see. It's… it's a terrible thing, lad, to know the will of God and to refuse it. But I was so afraid to fight. I thought I could hide behind my pulpit…maybe convince others to do what I knew God expected of *me*." Choking back a sob, he said, "I had my chance at that house, when you were only a little boy. That house…it broke me. I ran from it, and I never stopped. And I…I've hated myself ever since. Hated you, too, I suppose, because I saw you running *toward* the fight. Not like *I* did."

Greg felt a pang in his heart, a sharp twist. "Why are you telling me this?"

The elder Mitchell locked eyes with him. "Because now the house is due to come back, and you've got to do what I couldn't, son. You've got to face it. I know what your mother says—your sister. They only hear what the news tells them. But I *know* what you and your friends do. I know it's up to you, now, and I'm sorry for that. I'm sorry for a lot of things, Greg."

The man wept openly and unashamed, and Greg thought to do the same, until he heard the squawk of radio chatter and looked to the door. There, his sister was talking to two police officers, the three of them watching Greg with conspiratorial interest, already radioing for backup.

She did it, he thought. *She really called them.*

Seeing no use in hiding their intent any longer, the officers excused themselves from his grieving family and entered the room.

"Mr. Mitchell?" one began, his voice betraying a slight quaver, one hand on his holstered sidearm. "We'd like to ask you to step outside."

"No," his father weakly defended his son, and Greg was struck by the heartbreaking turnabout the man had made. "Leave him alone!"

"Mr. Mitchell," the other said, feigning calm. "Let's have a talk outside. Your dad doesn't need any more stress."

"Greg, *please*," Kathrine blurted, their weeping mother having returned to bawl loudly.

"Ma'am," an officer said, "stay back."

Greg didn't bother raising his hands as the officers edged ever closer.

"Mr. Mitchell, we're not asking you. We're telling you. Come with us. Don't make this harder on yourself."

"I won't," he replied, calm. "But I'm not coming with you."

The first officer huffed and reached for him. "That's it. You're—"

His hands passed through Greg's spectral form, as though grasping for smoke. The cop reeled back, bug-eyed and white with fear. His mother shrieked.

Greg took one last look at his family, those who had feared him most of his life, then offered a small grin to the officers. "Better luck next time," he said. Then, in a flash of ethereal light, he instantly returned to his corporeal form some four hundred miles away in Southern Illinois.

Greg Mitchell's eyes opened, and he gasped for breath. His body remained as he'd left it when he detached his soul to visit his father— sitting cross-legged on the floor of his hotel room, bare chest glistening with sweat, wearing nothing but a pair of pajama pants.

He sucked in oxygen, willing his body's functions to resume. He'd stayed away too long this time. Do that too often, and he might find his mortal shell unwilling to receive his immortal soul one day.

Greg stood on wobbly legs, tottering around the dark and sparse room, fumbling for the small refrigerator and the bottled water he kept there. He hurriedly screwed off the cap and tossed it away, then chugged, dribbling cold refreshment down his front.

Once he felt his heart rate resume, he recalled the address his father had shown him and the solemn charge he'd given him. In his mind, there was no question what must come next. Whatever his feelings were, whatever his fears—there was right and there was wrong.

His father had taught him that.

Greg reached for the burner phone on the counter and dialed out, still sipping his water.

A pretty voice answered, "Caliburn House."

"Alethea," he panted, catching a gasp. "It's Greg. Is Landon in? I… I think I need a doctor."

Bob Freeman & Greg Mitchell

Chapter Two

DETECTIVE DETRIPP MADE HIS WAY up the marble stair, hand gripping the mahogany rail every step of the way. Pausing every few steps, DeTripp wanted to curse the pacemaker that kept his heart in rhythm, but the alternative was less than appealing. Instead he spat inwardly at the insane wealth the occupants of Gottschalk Manor were swimming in. His salary with the Wabash PD was nothing to sneeze at, if you were to compare it to, say, what his cousin Pauley was pulling in down at the Gas Barn, but these Gottschalks? And what the hell kind of name was Gottschalk anyway? Probably old Nazi money. Yeah, that made sense. This place was nothing if not creepy.

DeTripp finally reached the top of the stairs and made his way down the hall, past the oil paintings of long dead creepy dudes and dames, a parade of sinister, but deceptively beautiful faces. He felt their eyes on him and he quickened his step, pacemaker be damned.

DeTripp spied Connors standing in a doorway ahead, unlit cigarette dangling from his Van Dyke framed lips. The kid dressed like a '40s gumshoe: long trench coat that was a tad too big for him and a weathered fedora, cocked just right and perched atop long, curly hair the color of an autumn sunset. The detective was envious, not just of Connors' good looks and charm, but of his youth and deep pockets. Not

Gottschalk deep, but a mite deeper than a cop's salary. *Get a grip, DeTripp,* he thought, *why am I fixating on dollar signs?* But he knew why. He just didn't want to give voice to it. His wife, God love her, had just come clean about their finances and her unfortunate addiction to playing the ponies down at Hoosier Park. They were sinking and fast. Thoughts of early retirement evaporated at the end of that conversation. Hell, they'd be lucky to have a roof over their heads if he didn't come up with something soon.

DeTripp parked himself next to the occult detective and took out a cigar to chew on while he worked. Smiling at the kid, he took a deep breath and prepared himself for the worst. See, if somebody brought Dr. Landon Connors in on this, that meant something weird was going down, and DeTripp didn't much care for weird.

"What's shakin', Doc?" DeTripp said, trying to muster up the sort of suave cool that TV cops oozed.

"There's water all over the bathroom," Connors replied calmly. "It looks like someone murdered an undine."

"A *what?*" DeTripp poked his head into the lavatory. Connors was right about the water—the floor was sopping in it. He could see it had spilled over from the clawfoot tub, a wrinkled knee rising up from inside.

"Gallows humor, detective," Connors said. He fumbled with his cigarette, then returned it to his mouth. Turning, he added, "You'll notice the wet marks on the carpet leading away from the washroom."

DeTripp knelt down and felt the carpet. He scowled, glancing back into the bathroom, eyes lingering on the wet floor, then again across the carpet. He rose slowly, a slight grunt escaping his lips.

"Almost dry," the detective remarked.

"Yes, but I brought along John Whitefeather," Connors said listlessly. DeTripp noticed he was staring back at the tub. "He's quite handy in situations like these, a real bloodhound. He was the one who took notice of the water in the hall. He followed the trail around the corner, where it ended at a dumbwaiter that was deposited on the ground floor."

DeTripp took notice of Connors leaning heavily on his cane, nursing that bum leg of his. He always meant to ask about it, but thought better of it on each occasion. Besides, the story would probably involve more of that weird stuff he'd rather not hear about.

"So who called you in?" DeTripp asked. To be honest, it was DeTripp who usually pulled that trigger. More than *usually*, actually, as in every single time of note. Rare was the occasion that Connors beat him to a crime scene.

"No one," Connors answered. "I had an appointment with the Lady of the Manor. When her manservant didn't answer the door, I… let myself in. I called out, received no reply, and followed the sound of running water to the scene before us."

"Is that a fact?" DeTripp gave Connors a quizzical look. His eyes darted across to the bathtub, its water turned off, though it was as full as full gets. "You turned the water off?"

"In a fashion," Connors replied. He lifted his hand up and spun his finger about. DeTripp caught his meaning and felt uneasy. Weirdness. He hated the weirdness. "I did a cursory search of the house, then called John in."

"Before me?" DeTripp all but barked.

"He has certain…talents that were necessary before the police disturbed things." Connors took the cigarette from his mouth and slid it back into the pack in his coat pocket. "But now that you're here, detective, perhaps we can examine the body. I have been patiently waiting to verify my concerns."

"I appreciate that at least," DeTripp said. "The waiting I mean."

"It's your case, detective," Connors said. "I'm here to offer my assistance."

DeTripp entered first, the water plopping as he gingerly made his way across the slick tile. The bathroom was big, bigger than his college apartment had been. Probably about the size of his future abode if he didn't get his finances squared away. He couldn't help but realize this room alone cost more than his entire house.

"Jesus," DeTripp grimaced as he stared down at the figure submerged in the tub.

"Christ had nothing to do with this," Connors said.

Staring back up at the two men was Madelena Gottschalk. Her eyes were wide open, her flesh shriveled, more from age than being submerged for two plus hours. DeTripp figured her to be a bit past ninety years, but when he had seen her at the City Gala a month back, he thought the old bird, still stunning despite her years, would sail past the century mark without effort. Her mind was sharp, her tongue sharper, and now she was a floater, her ticket cashed in for the great beyond.

Connors lowered himself slowly to one knee, oblivious to the standing water. The bathwater soaked into his wool Ermenegildo Zegna trousers, the wet rising up, changing the charcoal twill to a ruinous black. The occult detective pulled something out of his pocket, a vial of some sort and poured the clear liquid over the top of the deceased.

"Oh, hell no," DeTripp barked. "That's not going to contaminate my crime scene is it?"

"Absolutely not," Connors replied. "Now, silence please."

DeTripp didn't care much for the boy's tone, but he bit his lip just the same. He watched as Connors held his left hand out, palm and fingers wide, over the body. The air seemed to grow thicker, and DeTripp loosened his tie, looking around nervously. It felt like they were no longer alone. Then Connors spoke…

"Tsesuutromteeuqatiegrus. Tneimrod non maiaiuq."

A few bubbles rose from the bath, plopping as they touched the air. DeTripp took a step back. He didn't like this, not one bit. He'd experienced plenty of weird things around Connors, but as his nape hairs crawled, he knew this was about to reach a new level of weird. The air, once thick, was now even more so, and there was a strange scent wafting up from where Connors knelt, like the perfume his grandmother used to wear, lilacs or some such.

DeTripp was about to speak when that choice was robbed from him. His jaw dropped and, for the first time since childhood, he inwardly prayed to Jesus, Mary, and all the Saints he could remember. The water broke and Madelena Gottschalk rose up from the water, a flood of it spilling from the clawfoot tub, soaking Connors and the detective's worn-out leather oxfords. The old woman slowly turned her head toward Connors as DeTripp stumbled backwards, into the hall. His back came to rest against the wall, and he slid to the floor, his head swimming, his heart pounding so loud that he couldn't hear what Gottschalk was saying. Oh, he could see her lips moving as Connors held his hand out, placing it on the crown of her head. Then the crazy kid leaned in and kissed her full on the mouth. He lowered her back into the water and then stood awkwardly.

DeTripp concentrated on the plop of water as Connors navigated across the soaked lavatory. The young man was equally sodden, not that he seemed to notice. Connors had a faraway look about him, like he'd just cheated death. Who knew, maybe he had.

"What the hell was all that?" DeTripp asked.

"Never ask a question you don't want answered," Connors replied.

"Fair enough." DeTripp clumsily got up off the floor. He could breathe again. That was something. The air felt normal. The unseen presence from earlier was gone. But DeTripp's gut was none the better for it. "I don't suppose she told you what happened to her?"

"As I feared," Connors said, removing a cigarette from his pack, "she was murdered."

"Well, did the dearly departed happen to impart to you who did the deed? Because if so, that little tidbit of information might be useful." DeTripp took out his cigar, struck a match, lit it, and then Connors' smoke as well.

Connors took a long drag, then said, "I thought it was obvious."

"Oh, do tell?"

"Why my dear Detective DeTripp," Connors said, a smile creeping across his face, "the butler did it."

Connors turned and made his way down the hall. He began descending the marble stairs, and DeTripp followed. He spied two officers standing by the wide-open front door and a half dozen reporters clamoring to be let in.

"They do not budge from that threshold," he barked, his finger stabbing out like a cruel dagger.

DeTripp ignored the shouts from the newshounds, the sea of questions washing over him like a bad case of food poisoning. If there was anything he hated worse than the weird it was reporters and their incessant jawing.

"Where are we going?" the detective asked, still on Connors' heels. The kid hadn't even glanced at the reporters. He hit the entry hall and made straight for the back of the mansion, traversing the parlour and solarium without really taking notice. Opening the solarium door, they stepped out into the cool air of a mid-October twilight in bloom. They continued across the lawn, toward what looked like a mausoleum. *Great*, DeTripp thought, *more dead*. As they approached, Whitefeather stepped out of the tree line, pushing Karl Diener before him.

"Hello, Karl," Connors said.

"Dr. Connors," Diener replied solemnly. Diener was young, younger even than Connors. While he looked spooked, it was with a cool dispassion. He had the look of a man who knew his goose was cooked.

John Whitefeather held up a long chain, a skeleton key dangling from one of the links. DeTripp liked the Indian. He had a good nose. And while he was usually mixed up in the same business as Connors, John didn't give him the creeps like his more esoteric counterpart. John Whitefeather was good people, and honest. And while he never thought Connors outright lied to him, DeTripp always knew the kid was holding something back.

"Interesting," DeTripp said. He took the key from Whitefeather and looked it over. "Don't tell me this unlocks that," the detective said, motioning toward the crypt.

"What else?" John replied. "I caught Mr. Diener here fumbling with the lock. It's not been opened in more than a few years. He'd have been better served if he'd brought along a can of WD-40."

DeTripp chuckled, then turned to the Gottschalk manservant, slapping cuffs on him.

"Why'd you do it, son?" DeTripp asked over his shoulder. "Just to rob a few baubles from the dead?"

"I suggest we open the vault and bear witness to the young man's motivation," Connors said. He walked over to the crypt, leaning even heavier on his cane than before. He whispered some words and took hold of the ancient padlock, and it came away in his grasp. With a grimace, he pulled the iron gate open and rested his hands against the vault door.

"Murhclupesmutrepa," the occult detective said softly.

DeTripp bristled as the air turned electric, but it passed quickly, and he was curious to see what lay beyond. Connors pushed the tarnished brass doors inward and for the second time in one day Detective Ellis DeTripp's jaw hung open. Within the spacious crypt lay a single casket on a marble slab, dead center. Around the receptacle were chests of treasures unimaginable. Coins, jewels, swords, dusty old tomes, suits of armor. It was almost comical. It reminded DeTripp of the Phantom's vault in the old Lee Falk Sunday morning comic strip. It wasn't real. Surely.

"Jiminy-flippin'-Cricket," DeTripp said. He looked toward Diener. "Go big or go home, I guess." The detective took a step forward, standing next to Connors. "That dame ain't got no heirs," he said. "I guess that's why the kid made his play, before this all got divvied up in a will and he was left out in the cold."

"That reasoning will suffice," Connors said. His pocket buzzed, and the occult detective removed a flip phone from within his trench coat. He looked at the display and excused himself, stepping back out onto the lawn. DeTripp took one last look around with a sigh before he pulled the vault shut, swung the gate closed, and replaced the padlock.

Turning to Whitefeather and Diener, he said, "John, I really appreciate your assistance on this. You're a good egg."

"Always a pleasure, Detective," the stoic Whitefeather responded.

DeTripp looked over toward Connors who was animatedly talking into his cell. "If you're not careful, that one will be the death of you."

"He is the Magician & the Exorcist, the axle of the wheel, and the cube in the circle..." the Indian said. His eyes focused on Connors, as well. The occult detective put away his phone and limped across the lawn to rejoin them.

"Trouble back at Caliburn," he said.

John looked concerned and asked, "Something I can help with, old friend?"

"Not this time, John," Connors replied. "It's Mitchell."

"I see," the Indian said.

"Well, isn't this all nice and freaking cryptic," DeTripp spat. He tugged hard on Diener's arm, and the manservant grimaced.

"Sorry, Detective," Connors said. "Evil never rests." He turned and began walking away, adding over his shoulder, "If you need a statement, I should be back by the first of November, give or take."

DeTripp dropped his chewed-up cigar onto the ground and snuffed it out with his heel, returning his attention to his prisoner. Then, as an afterthought, he called out to Connors—

"Landon, you never did tell me why you'd stopped by to see Ms. Gottschalk."

Connors stopped and faced the detective.

"It was the matter of her Will," he said. He took out a fresh cigarette and lit it off the one now spent. "It seems she was to leave everything to Caliburn House."

"Well, I'll be damned," DeTripp spat as he watched Connors leave for parts unknown.

Chapter Three

GREG SPOTTED THE CENTURY-old County Courthouse and turned his dinged-up, faded blue Dodge Ram work truck west onto Hill Street, driving past the castle-like fire station, the *Italianate* and Federal architecture of weathered but attractive homes, the historic James Ford property, and the Romanesque Carnegie Library before pulling up in front of the imposing Second Empire façade of the legendary Caliburn House. He shut off the ancient engine and blew out a sigh, facing down the forbidding abode. While he considered its occupants among his closest friends, Greg could barely tolerate the house itself. Just being near its mouth set his soul on edge, and he couldn't fathom how Connors could live in the blasted place and not lose his mind. There was a taint to this particular patch of Earth, some spiritual cancer that Landon Connors had either tamed, ignored—or become so intimate with as to not notice.

Nevertheless, Greg noticed, and did not travel here to rural Indiana lightly.

After muttering a prayer of praise, centering on the goodness of God in an effort to realign his spirit with the Light before venturing into the darkness, Greg reached for the duffel in the passenger seat and removed himself from the Dodge. His boots crunched on rocks until he drew near to ascend the steps. He raised a hand to knock when the door opened of its own. His breath caught for a moment, until he saw the pretty young thing standing on the other side.

Alethea Hill leaned against the frame, arms folded, head at a tilt to allow thick, dark locks to cascade across her slender shoulder, a mischievous smirk playing across her lovely face. "Well, well, look what the cat dragged in."

Greg adjusted the duffel strap on his shoulder, shifting its weight, and blushed around a grin.

"I heard that," an annoyed voice muttered at their feet, and Greg glanced down to see a black cat working his way between Alethea's ankles.

The woman nodded to the feline. "Boo heard you coming."

Greg smirked. "Hey, Boo."

"Mitchell."

His interest waning, Connors' familiar slunk away, disappearing into the maddening halls of the house, and Greg knew he would have to follow. Alethea stepped aside, granting him entrance. "He's in the study," she said, her tone losing its playful quality, moving on to business.

Greg crossed the threshold, and she gently closed the door behind him. "Has he got anything?"

She bobbed a shrug and presented the path. "See for yourself."

The enchanting assistant led Greg to a set of double doors and opened them onto Landon Connors' inner sanctum, revealing the wicked man himself. Presently, Connors busied about his expansive library, his familiar trench coat and hat removed, collar unbuttoned, sleeves rolled up haphazardly. Spread out on his large table and about the floor were various tomes and loose papers, forming a sort of maze of lore. Connors scratched at his goatee as he read the text in hand, mumbling to himself.

"He's been like this for *hours*," Alethea whispered with a mild sense of aggravation.

Greg frowned and glanced to Connors' faithful associate for support, but she withdrew from the study to attend to matters elsewhere. Alone, Greg faced the library and crossed over. "Hey."

Connors didn't bother looking up. "Mitchell."

Greg cleared off a spot on the chair in the corner and deposited his duffel, careful to step over the patterns of photos, newspaper clippings and open grimoires cluttering the floor. Seeing so much raw data was overwhelming, as Greg never fancied himself much of a detective. That was Connors' strength, whereas Greg was more of a hammer. His education was in demonology, studying the natures and habits of hell's own—so as to better send them back beyond the Veil. Despite Connors' best efforts to train him over the few years they'd known one another, he'd not taken so well to spellcasting and rune reading and *research*. Endless hours of research.

He put his hands on his hips and looked around at the gargantuan task, trying not to sound exasperated so soon into the case. "Want me to jump in somewhere?"

Connors continued to murmur under his breath, then momentarily set down the book he was holding to fish in his pocket for a cigarette. With a snap of his fingers, a small flame ignited the tip of the cancer stick, and the occult detective took a long, anxious pull before exhaling his stresses. "What have you gotten me into this time?"

Greg gestured to the explosion of paper at their feet and chuckled. "Clearly more than I realized."

Aggravated, Connors sucked the cigarette dry and extinguished the butt before folding over the table and the large book that lay open. "After this, no more favors. You *owe* me."

Greg held out his hands in mock surrender, then joined his cantankerous friend. "So what are we looking at?"

"Records from Franklin County, where your mysterious house rests—"

"Wait, that's in Arkansas. How did you get these to Indiana?"

"Teleportation. Better than e-mail." Connors rubbed his swollen eyes and grumbled. "If you don't mind, I've been at this for two days. We can either retrace my steps or jump to what I've learned. Hallowe'en draws nearer, and time is running out."

Greg smirked. "Sorry. You were saying?"

A mild bow. "Thank you." Lighting another cigarette—this one he consumed more slowly—he flipped through marked pages, barely giving Greg a chance to read. "Your father was right. The house has been appearing in this one spot every thirty years."

"For how long?"

"There was a flood that destroyed most of the old records—but there are reports as early as 1890 of this occurrence, so…"

"Wow. What's there now?"

Connors slapped the book closed. "Nothing. I followed the paper trail—the *county* owns the land now. It's an empty lot. Fenced off. Civilization has grown up around it, but they stopped trying to build on that patch of land in 1960, when the surveyor was found turned inside out."

Greg swallowed. "Oh."

"The house may only appear on the 31st every thirty years, but in the meantime, there are still dozens of reported phenomena. Missing persons, strange weather that only seems to affect that area—lightning storms, rain of frogs, the usual—bizarre noises, unsettling smells."

"And only on that property?"

"Only on the property," Connors confirmed immediately. "That hasn't been much comfort to the neighbors. Most people give the lot a wide berth. The entire street is practically abandoned, if the kindly receptionist at the Franklin County Courthouse is to be believed."

Greg instinctively glanced to his trusty duffel, mentally perusing its contents. Inside were his silver short sword, faithful .357 Ruger, and odds and ends of charms and sacraments. They'd gotten him out of a lot of scrapes, but suddenly seemed inadequate for the task ahead.

"So," he began, almost afraid to ask, "what do you think?"

"A better question is how your father got involved."

Stuffing his hands in his jeans, Greg moseyed about the room, mindful of the mess. "Yeah... I asked around on that front. Didn't get very far. There's so much I don't know about the man. I guess I never really knew him at all."

At last, Connors set aside his preoccupation and relaxed. "How are you doing?"

Greg released a tired, half-hearted snicker. "How am I *supposed* to be doing?"

"Never an easy thing, the bond between father and son."

Connors, Greg knew, spoke from experience.

"Yeah. Guess so." Stifling a sudden urge to cry or scream, Greg scratched his cheek and cleared his throat. "This house then. Theories?"

"Of course."

"Care to share them with the class, professor?"

Connors grinned devilishly. "My best guess? How do you feel about parallel dimensions?"

Greg spun about and locked eyes with the occult detective. Once he was sure the wizard wasn't joking, he slumped and fished out his keys. "*I'll* drive."

Chapter Four

CONNORS WAS PERCHED IN the passenger seat of Greg's faded blue Ram, fedora pulled down low, shadowing his face from the glare of oncoming traffic. A SideKick book light was clamped to the lapel of the detective's suit jacket, its pin light snaking outward to illuminate the thick, leather bound journal in his lap. A glance was all Greg needed to divine the sourcebook his former mentor was devouring—a Liber Monstrorum, one of several volumes painstakingly curated by the hermetic social club that had counted Connors' lineage as members going back at least two centuries.

Greg had never actually joined the Order of the Sacred Hart. By the time he'd entered Connors' orbit, the Order was reduced, by and large, to Connors alone. Oh, one might consider Landon's assistant, Thea Hill, as an initiate, possibly even the detective's man Friday, Brooks Autry, but the Order had seemed to fall away with the death of Connors' father a few years back. Greg knew that Connors viewed the Order as a phoenix, that it would rise from the ashes of its decline in the not-too-distant future, but the ghost of Ashton Connors and the disbanded Order clung to the occult detective more like a proverbial albatross.

Greg navigated his battered work truck across the narrow back roads of Indiana, past harvested fields of corn and wheat, where copses of old growth trees still clung to the banks of twisting creeks and streams. He pulled the truck to the side of the road somewhere just north of Lafayette. A sign announced they were near a place named Battle Ground, and that symbolism was not lost on the demonologist. He roused Connors from his reading and motioned across a field. Corn stalks still stood, crisp and harvest gold, a few dozen yards back, and there a herd of deer grazed, their heads up, eyes wide, and ears alert to danger.

"A good omen," the detective said. He opened his door slowly, confidently. Leaning heavily on his cane, he did not wait for Mitchell to join him. He stalked out across the rutted field until he stood in the deer's midst. Greg followed more cautiously, though he could feel the energy that Connors projected.

That it suddenly seemed as bright as day passed unnoticed. Greg came to stand slightly behind the detective, basking in the warmth of the channeled magic that Connors drew out of the earth. He could feel it swell up from the ground, from an underground waterway that coursed with an ancient power. Greg calmed himself, as he had been taught, and allowed his spirit to loose itself that he might see the spectacle in its true magnificence.

Astral threads, thin like gossamer, stretched out in a circle, enveloping the herd and the two visitors. Like strands of pure gold, this magical construct pulsed with an undeniable rhythm that was seemingly alive, like a thundering heartbeat. Greg watched as Connors gently coursed white, spectral light from the deer's bodies. He gathered it into his hands, then absorbed it.

"May the Gods always stand between us and harm," Connors said as he reached out and took Mitchell's hand, "in all the empty places we must walk."

Greg felt a portion of the white light enter him, and it pulled his astral form back down into his physical body, and the spell was broken. The deer scattered to the wind, leaving the two men alone in the field.

"I feel better about our quest now, my friend," Landon said. He motioned for Greg to join him in returning to the truck. Overhead, a crow circled, soon joined by another. They descended ahead of the men, one landing on the hood of the truck, the other on the roof. Connors stopped dead in his tracks.

"What is it?" Greg hissed. His hand went instinctively to the rosary in his pocket.

"I spoke too soon," Connors replied. "What do you want with us, Maelfix?" the detective barked. His left hand made a protective gesture, subtle, but not without power.

"Herd magic," one of the crows cawed. "Desperate, Landon has become."

"You have no power here, hellspawn," Connors spat. He raised his cane, pointing it toward the crows. Mitchell moved in close. While magic was not his *forté*, consorting with demons was. He began reciting the Lord's Prayer and mentally constructing a circle of protection, calling upon the Archangels from their Watchtowers to fortify the esoteric sphere.

"Fear, I sense," the crow continued. "The sparrow road is far from here, but not as the crow flies. When the host has gathered in the house of broken shutters, then the eye will be opened and the old man quake."

"Your words are empty," Mitchell charged. He crossed himself, then said, "Turn back the evil upon my foes; in your faithfulness destroy them. Freely will I offer you sacrifice; I will praise your name, Lord, for its goodness, because from all distress you have rescued me, and my eyes look down upon my enemies. Glory be to the Father as it was in the beginning. Save your servant, who trusts in you, my God. Let me find in you, Lord, a fortified tower in the face of the enemy."

Connors reached out and placed his hand on Greg's chest, forcing the young man to take a step back as the detective stepped forward gingerly. Though his limp was prominent, the cane did not waver from its raised position.

"Fear?" Connors said. "From the likes of you?" Another limp forward. "Maelfix, you know me better than that. No, the reverse is true, for you have showed your hand. We are poised at the head of our journey, but you have come too quickly to ward us off. It is you who fear, you who sense the righteousness of our crusade."

"In the silent well, beneath the dead cock's wing, a worm will be eaten, and it will taste like bitter fruit," the crow squawked. "But in the windowless room, where the giant sleeps and the goat is bespelled by the Dagger Head Box, there is a black mark drawn in a librarian's blood, and that sign shall be an unraveling and a harbinger that the weatherman is not always on fire."

The crow flapped its wings and rose up above the truck, its companion following suit. They began to circle, slowly rising higher into the darkening sky. Mitchell and Connors watched as black clouds rolled in, consuming the light of day, and delivering a thunderous torrent, lightning coursing in those heavens like vengeance given form.

"You will lie among dead flowers," the crow cawed as it flew into the storm. "Dirt shall be your just reward."

"What in the name of all that's holy?" Greg thrust his arm up for protection as hailstones began to pummel him and Connors. The wind raged, rocking the Dodge as they climbed into the truck for cover.

"Discretion is the better part of valor," Connors said. "The road beckons us to shelter."

"I can barely see," Greg said. A tree, uprooted, fell into the field. A host of blackbirds took flight from it, diving back into the safety of the trees that held firm, though they swayed and bent with nature's fury.

"Drive!" Connors bellowed, and Greg turned the key and sped off.

Before them was an oppressive black, like a rain-laden thundercloud had settled on the country road. The wind howled. The thunder crashed. Hail and rain continued in relentless torrent. Still Greg pressed on, desperate to keep the Ram on the road, his nerves on edge.

"Can't you do something?" he asked, frantically looking toward his former mentor. Connors was fast asleep. Multiple wet, slapping sounds drew Greg's attention back toward the road ahead. The windshield was being covered by tarot cards, spat by the wind and rain.

"Wh-What the—?"

Greg was confused. He looked to Connors, then back to the windshield. The cards, glued to the windshield, were all face out, creating a sea of hermetic rose crosses…save one. Mitchell looked closely, but the card was obscured. It fluttered there, dead center of his field of vision. He lowered the driver-side window and the truck became filled with a deafening roar. Reaching out, he grabbed at the card, which continually escaped his grasp until at last he peeled it free. Pulling it inside, he stared at the card—the Tower: symbol of war, ruin, of beliefs being torn asunder.

"Blessed be the Lord our God who hath given us the Symbol Signum," Connors said, stirring. Mitchell turned to him, but when he saw Connors recoil in fear, curling up protectively, he snapped his attention back to the road ahead. Coming straight for them was a crow, massive in size, diving out of the black cloud like a missile. It struck the windshield, shattering it, its bloodied and broken body falling on the seat between them. Greg tried to slam on the brakes, but there was no pedal…

Then the whole world came to a violent stop and his vision was full of stars.

The impact threw Greg forward into the steering wheel. He felt a hand roughly grab his shoulder. His foot was still jammed down on the brake. He felt a trickle of blood running down his forehead and across his cheek.

"Are you alright?" Connors asked.

Mitchell blinked. The sky was clear. It was night time. He shut off the engine as Connors opened the door and stepped out onto the highway, rolling forests on either side of the road.

"Greg?" Connors said again.

"Yeah," Mitchell replied. "Yeah, I'm fine, what—?"

He climbed out of the truck and walked around to the passenger side. The front fender was caved in and covered in blood. Connors was kneeling beside the road, lifting the head of a large stag off the asphalt. Its hind quarter was a ruined mess of broken bone, ripped flesh, and gore. Connors looked up at Greg and shook his head. Then with a sudden jerk, he snapped the deer's neck.

"What happened to the crow?" Greg muttered, still groggy from his impact with the steering wheel.

"Crow?" Connors said. He stood up and lit a cigarette. "What are you talking about?" He took a long drag. "Are you sure you're okay?"

Mitchell was about to answer when he noticed something lying on the edge of the berm. He bent and picked it up. His head swam, and he staggered back against the truck, the deer's blood smearing his jeans. In his hand was a tarot card, the back depicting the Golden Dawn Rosy Cross Lamen. Turning it over slowly, Greg blinked as he processed the image: two figures falling from a burning tower struck down by a lightning bolt from the sky, surrounded by cabalistic trees. He let the card fall from his hand.

"Where are we?" Greg asked, a settling calm coming over him.

"We're just outside Alix," Connors said.

Mitchell's eyes drifted toward the road sign—Sparrow Lane, it read.

"We're here, then?" he said, eyes glued on the sign.

"Just about," Connors replied. He finished the smoke and ground it out in the gravel berm. "Greg, something's not right here. What is it?"

"Can't you feel it?" Mitchell asked. His eyes turned away from the sign, looking south across the treetops. He focused on the dark clouds on the horizon.

"There's a storm coming," he added.

Connors followed his former student's gaze, the distant lightning reflected in his eyes.

"We'd best to it then," Connors said.

"I reckon so."

Chapter Five

THE DODGE RAM COUGHED and grumbled, winding down Sparrow Lane. The backroad was sparsely populated with fading, turn-of-the-century homes, though newer subdivisions branched off from the main road leading down into cleared-out valleys. From here, Greg saw porch lights, and with his window rolled down, he could hear the excited chatter of trick-or-treaters. Children dressed as goblins and ghouls raced through yards, passing by gleefully observing jack-o'-lanterns, beseeching treats from friendly neighbors. Small clusters of adults were gathered in driveways, nestled under blankets, warming themselves by portable fire pits. Radios sat in the beds of parked pick-ups, loudly blaring novelty monster songs, adding a campy soundtrack to the evening.

Greg smiled bittersweetly at the festivities, wondering if either man in the cab of his beat-up truck had ever known such innocent pursuits. Surely not, for both Mitchell and Landon Connors had been inducted quite early on into the darker realities of the macabre. But, oh, to be a child again on this night. To don a terrifying visage—not in the tribute to Evil that Greg's own parents believed Hallowe'en signified, but in defiance *against* it. To make light of it, to brave a night filled with pretend monsters and declare to the shadows, "I am not afraid of you."

Magic of the best kind. The purest kind. Greg craved that simple childlike clarity again, on this night of monsters and mystery. Perhaps he and his companion had delved too deeply into the darkness to ever hold such hope again. He prayed that weren't so.

As they climbed up a knoll, leaving behind the warm lights of welcoming doorstops and rambunctious make-believe devils, Greg supposed they would discover soon enough.

With some effort, the truck crested the hill, finally coming to a wheezing halt in front of the fenced-in field at the neglected end of Sparrow Lane. The Ram gave up its ghost, and Greg worried he wouldn't be able to resurrect it when the time came to leave this accursed place. Assuming they were able to leave at all.

Worn out from their twelve-hour drive, he and Connors climbed out of the truck, sighing and stretching and groaning from the exhaustive trip—though Greg reckoned he'd been absent for most of it. His startling vision of the crows, the rains, of the demon Maelfix disturbed him greatly, distracting him from what they had come to do. Had he dreamed the whole thing? No, he'd known dreams—even vivid and bizarre ones, but this was real. Maybe it hadn't happened on this plane, but in some dread dimension he'd been visited by a demon.

Had his father met those same terrors? If so, no wonder the man fled with his faith in tatters. Who could stand against something so unspeakably wicked?

Connors cleared his throat, spat, then rummaged about in his coat for a cigarette. The man hobbled to the fence, cane tucked under one arm as he lit his smoke. Greg smirked at the rumpled detective and considered he was fortunate to know at least *one* man fool enough to face hell.

The friends arrived at the fence. Beyond it lay a vacant lot, nothing but the stone foundation of some long-forgotten house. The weeds were tremendous, promising bugs and snakes and a sundry collection of woodland creatures lurking within. Yet, upon second thought, the place was impossibly quiet. The air was thick and musty, like an old attic. The wind did not blow, though dark, flickering clouds circled overhead like hungry predators.

A shiver raced down Mitchell's arms, raising the hairs there.

"Must be the place," he grumbled, nerves on edge.

Connors nodded thoughtfully, taking long pulls off his cancer stick, eyeing the overgrown lot. Then he faced his partner. "Shall we?"

Greg nodded and leapt to the fence, scaling it, carefully navigating the rusted barbed wire at the top, then landing solidly on the other side. He chuckled and waved Connors forward. "You next. I'll catch you."

"Hah," Landon said without humor, then waved his hand, mumbling an incantation. The links in the fence grew red hot, then molten. Like limp spaghetti noodles, they slipped away, opening a small portal that Connors could pass through if he ducked.

"Showoff," Greg said.

Connors eased onto the lot, joining Mitchell in the weeds. "Hallowe'en is nearly over," Greg noted. "Doesn't give us much time to prepare."

"But prepare for *what* is the greater dilemma. By all accounts, the house should be here by now."

Greg took the flashlight from his coat pocket and switched it on, casting its light back and forth across the silent field. "Feel anything yet?"

"My back hurts from sitting in the truck so long, and I've got to whiz like a race horse, if that's what you mean."

Greg smirked, and the quiet soon overtook the men as they searched. All the while, Mitchell considered his ominous vision. Connors, himself, had warned him of these types of visitations during the years Greg sat under his tutelage. It was a natural side effect of slipping off one's mortal coil to take walkabouts in the heavenlies. No way for a soul to go traipsing in the shadow realms between Life and Death and not *attract* things. Greg had always been careful to guard himself against such preternatural hitchhikers, but had his luck finally run out? Perhaps this vision was only a byproduct of his natural sight realigning with his *spiritual* eyes. If that were so, if the Veil was finally rent aside for good… Well, one could go mad if made to observe the full truth of the world all the time.

Greg suddenly worried what his future held if he continued on this path, and he remembered his vision. *You will lie among dead flowers*, the crow had prophesied. *Dirt shall be your just reward.*

"Hey, uh…Landon," Mitchell began. "About, ah, earlier. In the truck—"

Connors stopped, supporting himself on his cane, lifting his chin in patient wisdom. "At last we come to it."

"Yeah. Look, I saw something. In my vision there was a—"

A rustle in the weeds, where there had been no sign or movement before. Connors jerked his chin at the sound. Greg slipped free his .357 Ruger revolver, alert. Landon quickly lifted his hand and snapped his fingers, casting a spark that shone like an orange flare, pushing back the black night. In the flickering light, Greg scanned the area for activity.

"See anything?" he mumbled, breath leaving his body in frosty puffs.

Connors shook his head but did not speak.

A shrill warble—something more akin to a Valkyrie's war cry than any natural animal call—split the silence as a shape catapulted from the tall grass, aimed right for Mitchell. Arms extended, claws flexed, the bent creature flew at him, screeching. Greg gasped and stepped back, leveling his six-shooter and firing twice, driving two iron rounds through the darkened form. The thing squealed and tumbled into the weeds. Almost instantly, Mitchell and Connors huddled around it to survey the fresh corpse by Landon's witch-light.

The dead female lay twisted, bare feet and hands curled into blackened eagle talons. Purple veins throbbed beneath moon-white skin. A full set of lion-like fangs protruded from a sallow face.

Connors pursed his lips. "Vampires."

As though the word were a signal, the barren lot came alive with stirrings. This time, the occult detective drew his own revolver, and the two hunters pressed together back to back. Connors discarded his cane to his side, and Mitchell withdrew the silver short sword from its sheath on his thigh.

"Have at thee, devil-kin!" Connors proclaimed to weeds that rippled and rumbled. Growls filled the once-quiet hush, followed by wet snaps and snarls.

"I've had conversations with vampires," Greg huffed, eyes darting left to right, waiting for an attack. "These are more like animals!"

"Starved, I'd wager," Connors offered over his shoulder, his voice betraying a slight waver of panic.

A hiss from the left startled Greg into action. He bolted to his side, just in time to see a set of fangs and claws falling on him. He swung his pistol to fire, but the beast was too fast, slapping his hand away and lowering his mouth to feed.

"Mitchell!" Connors cried, firing a single bullet into the vampire's temple. It gave a jerk of the head and toppled sideways to squirm on the ground, gathering itself for another attack.

Outraged and frightened, Greg hollered and brought his short sword down with a thunderous chop, decapitating the twitching vampire, soaking the hard-packed earth with stale blood.

And, like that, the battle was on. Vampires scurried from every shadow, snapping massive jaws, flexing onyx claws. Mitchell and Connors whirled and fired at differing hemispheres, beating back the first wave. In no time, their six-shooters ran dry. Greg didn't bother reloading—the fight was too thick. In one fluid motion, he slid his gun back on his belt and took the sword in both hands, stepping out and away from his partner to hack and slash more freely.

With Connors' concentration broken by the surprise attack, his magical illumination began to fade. In the descending dark, with no discernible moonlight to guide them, thanks to the gathering storm above, Greg didn't have the luxury of precision. He swung wildly, feeling his holy blade cleave meat and bite bone. Arms fell away, fingers and parts of shoulders chipped off his attackers. He caught a vampire by the cheek, shredding his lower jaw, but still the beast's tongue unfurled like a dripping tentacle, reaching for him all the same.

In the melee, Greg did his best to count their adversaries—*Seven? A dozen?*—but they moved so fast, glowing eyes streaking like neon in the gloom, that he couldn't properly distinguish one monster from the next. He simply knew— "There's too many of them!"

Connors hurriedly reloaded, carefully picking his shots. "Brute force won't win this day," he said, then dropped to his knees. "Cover me, won't you?"

Greg sputtered. "C-*Cover* you?!"

The occult detective removed his hat and crossed his legs. Taking deep, calm breaths, he moved his hands about in the air, murmuring incantations. Greg huffed and leapt forward, lashing out with a wide arc of silver just as a vampire sought to devour the praying wizard. The blade sank into throat, and the vampire wrenched himself free, gurgling as a red waterfall spewed from his gaping neck wound.

A second vampire clambered onto his back, encircling its wiry legs around Greg's torso. Mitchell grunted and twisted, unable to dislodge his assailant. With greedy fervor, the creature tore at Greg's collar, prying back his jacket and shirt to expose his neck for the feasting.

Only discovering too late the small cross tattooed there.

The menace twisted against the holy icon as if pepper had been thrown in its nose, and Greg bared his teeth in defiance. Still swiping at the vampires before him, he loudly recited, "Praise the Lord! Praise God in His sanctuary; Praise Him in His mighty expanse. Praise Him for His mighty deeds; Praise Him according to His excellent greatness."

The ghoul hissed and bucked, finally releasing its hold on Mitchell. With sizzling hands, the night stalker fell to the ground, and Greg swung with deadly accuracy, cleanly removing the vampire's screaming head from its shoulders.

Grinning savagely, Greg gave a flick of his blade, painting the nearby weeds in red excess, then snapped at his partner, "Landon, any time you'd like to join in, feel free. What are you *doing* anyway?"

"Feeling," he panted, then resumed his arcane words. "There's a connection…here… I sense a bond—"

Greg only half-heard his former mentor, as he danced around the man in a circle, defending every flank. He was exhausted, breathing hard as the vampires bit and clacked their teeth—but did not press their advantage. They were testing his defenses. Toying with him.

"Landon…"

The ghouls traded silent looks with one another, communicating as a pack. Greg brandished his sword as a ward, offering his own prayers to his own God.

"Invisible threads," Connors mumbled, then his eyes shot open. "I see it now! These beasts are bound to a single purpose. A single will!"

The slobbering beasts hunkered into a crouch, growling as their eyes blazed. Greg's breathing was sharp and pained as he gasped in fearful expectation.

Connors moved his hands about in the air, forming brilliant configurations of light. "They are… on a psychic leash—a tether… If I could only—"

The vampires barked and charged as one, flailing and biting. Greg flexed his fingers around the blade and raised it, ready to fight to the bitter end. "*Come on!*" he dared them.

His heart shuddered with terror when, at just the moment the vampires took to the air, sailing straight for him, they were jerked taut from behind, crashing to the grass in a near-simultaneous collision.

Mitchell blinked the sweat out of his eyes, gaping as the vampires groveled on the ground, coming to their senses, looking to one another in surprise. At this, Connors stood, hand held high with his fingers splayed, light emanating forth.

"Now *I* hold your leash, curs."

The vampires roared their protest, readying for another strike, only this time Landon Connors made a tight fist and the monsters clutched at their throats, dropped to their knees and howled to the night sky.

Flames erupted from their eyes and mouths, stealing their voices until, at the end, they exploded into smoldering embers.

Spent, Connors tipped forward without benefit of his cane, but Greg was there to catch his friend. "Easy! I got you."

Connors braced against Mitchell's arm, giving his jacket sleeve a good pat. "Let's hope that's the worst of it, shall we? And don't forget—"

"I owe you," Greg huffed, rolling his eyes before breaking out into a grin. "Yeah, yeah."

"A pity about the vampires," a deep, melodious voice courting a British accent addressed the weary warriors. A short, lean man—elderly, with a pointed bald head and wizened eyes behind wire-rim glasses— calmly strolled through the weeds. He wore a dark suit, as did the five hardened men in his company. "They had their uses."

Connors stiffened with recognition. He snatched his cane from the ground and snarled. "*You.* What the bloody hell are you doing here?"

The British man chuckled. "Surely you didn't believe you were the only ones interested in this rather peculiar house, did you, Dr. Connors?"

Greg leaned closer, whispering. "You know who these guys are?"

"Yes," he replied heavily. "I know." Connors glowered at the well-dressed men and declared through bared teeth: "The Order of the Black Spire."

Chapter Six

"I LOVE YOU."

Greg Mitchell was in a fog, both literally and figuratively. Somewhere, like a distant echo, there was pain, but it was buried deep, just like this memory had been. He looked at the young woman in front of him as she became more substantial and the room around them began to take form. Mary Alice Giordano, though she preferred MAlice or MAGs. He had loved her once, long ago. He loved her still. He was standing in the doorway of the apartment they'd shared in Mountain Rest. His duffle bag was on the floor at his feet, a backpack slung over his shoulder. They contained all his earthly possessions. At least the ones he meant to hold onto. MAlice was crying. Couldn't forget that. It was carved into his brain, jagged and as fresh as the day he'd said he was leaving.

"I love you too," Greg replied. He had no choice. He was playing out the memory. His eyes darted out the window. In the foggy soup he could make out a figure being drug across a field, but then it was gone, and he couldn't remember why that might matter. He was in the moment.

"But...?" MAlice snapped. She was furious. Greg remembered it all too well. The distant pain, the echo, was nothing compared to this wound. "Damn you, Greg Mitchell, we have a life here, you and me. We're building something, and you want to throw it all away on some fool's errand!"

She grabbed a coffee cup from the counter and hurled it across the room. Greg watched it spin in slow motion, the words "MONEY CAN'T BUY YOU HAPPINESS, BUT IT CAN BUY BOOKS, WHICH IS ESSENTIALLY THE SAME THING" tumbling over and over until the mug glanced off his head and shattered against the wall in a thousand porcelain shards.

He didn't feel it any more than he felt the echo of pain that was out there, somewhere in the fog.

"You don't understand," he repeated, unable to alter the course of this memory. He was a puppet, and the past controlled the strings. "I need help. Dr. Connors can…"

"Go to hell," she wailed. "Both of you!" She stormed out of the room, slamming the bedroom door behind her. "Go to hell and rot!" she exclaimed. They were the last words she had spoken to him. Three days after their dust-up he was staying at Caliburn House under the tutelage of Landon Connors, Occult Detective, and she was lying in a ditch, bleeding out, her F-150 wrapped around a telephone pole. She'd been drinking. By the time the ambulance arrived, she was gone.

The fog became thicker, and Greg Mitchell was still in Mountain Rest, but he was younger, barely a teenager, and he was experiencing a different sort of pain. He was in the basement of his family home, kneeling before a picture of Jesus Christ. That image was burned into his brain. Christ was aglow, and from his chest burned the Sacred Heart. He winced as a jolt of pain coursed through his body, and Greg remembered all too well where this memory's roots lay.

Greg was shirtless, oblivious to the damp chill of the basement. His father saw to that. The scourge, a knotted length of hemp rope and leather, thin and whip-like, lashed out, again and again. Welts were raised. There were bruises and cuts. But none of that was as painful as the psychological damage that was being inflicted.

"No son of mine," his father ranted, each word punctuated by a lash, "will consort with demons!" The beatings were never bad enough to land him in the hospital, and his mother would always tenderly address his wounds after, but the scars they left were always with him, no matter how deep he buried them.

But then the fog returned, and the basement dissolved, and he was looking out across the Mississinewa River. Connors was nearby, leaning on the twisted cane that had once belonged to the infamous Aleister Crowley. Connors seemed perplexed. They were at a place called the Flats, where the water was shallow and the riverbed a massive slab of limestone all the way out to a tiny island where local teens gathered to smoke dope and cigarettes and drink beer they'd swiped from someone's old man's fishing cooler. Greg remembered this night well. It was the last he'd spent as Connors' student. It was the night he decided that Connors' path was not for him.

"Blood," Connors muttered, "so much blood."

There was no blood, Greg remembered. His mentor was out of his head, having ingested a strange mixture of mushrooms and psychotropic plants. Connors was examining a crime scene that didn't exist, not in this reality anyway. Greg looked away, back toward Somerset, the small town's lights peeking through the trees. There, in the soupy fog, Greg saw the strange figure again, being drug toward what he thought was a farmhouse, but then it was gone, as Connors drew him back to the memory being played out.

"They were torn apart," he stammered, "by some kind of… animal, ferocious, and… No, not an animal…" He staggered across the gravel cul-de-sac and grabbed Greg by the shoulders, shaking him. "A vampire," he shouted. "The undead stalk the shadows of Somerset."

"You're losing it," Greg said to him, pushing Connors away.

"Don't you see?" Connors said. "There's been a divergence in the timeline." His eyes were as wide as saucers. He dug into his trench coat and drew out a coin, flipping it into the air. "In this timeline," he continued, snatching the coin out of midair and slapping it onto the back of his hand, "the coin comes up heads, but in that other timeline," he waved his hand over the coin.

"I know," Greg said, "it comes up tails."

"No," Connors smiled. "It was never a coin at all." He moved his hand to reveal a stone, wet and glistening. He brushed it away, onto the ground. "Look around you," he said, "the possibilities are endless. But the power, the magic to do such a thing, to alter fate…"

Suddenly Connors became sullen. There was so much pain in his eyes. He looked at Greg, and Greg understood now what he didn't then, that Connors was seeing more than alternate realities and parallel universes. His third eye, ripped wide open, saw the inner workings, the gears and levers, of creation itself.

"There are answers here, within the quantum mechanics of this strange new world," he opined, "and questions. So many more questions. We are operating in a reality that is fluid and transitory. There is no foundation. We are on a trajectory that leads us beyond the extraordinary and into truly cosmic realms, that not only shatters the very fabric of our reality, but of the realities of every other province of the multiverse."

His words frightened Greg, in ways he could not express. This was madness, the young man thought. His mentor had crossed the line from wisdom to psychosis, or so Greg had felt. Now he was far less sure. Another sound led his eyes back into the fog, where the echo of pain lay in wait, and where, again, he saw that strange procession, the smoky figure, suspended between two silhouettes, drug toward the steps of a weathered porch, but then it was gone again, and so too was Greg Mitchell, enveloped once more by the murky haze.

And then Greg was in a cabin, his breath blending with the scattering effluvium. It was small and intimate. On a desk lay a worn, leather journal, a stack of books, grimoires from the look of them, and his .357 Ruger, a splay of silver bullets strewn about haphazardly, as well. This was no memory, he thought, this was something else altogether.

A sound drew him to the door, as he found himself again a puppet of this, whatever it was. He opened the cabin door and stared out across a frozen expanse. A man was approaching, dressed against the cold. He was wearing a green parka with a Wisconsin Conservation Officer patch on the sleeve.

"Howdy," the man said. He was young, his face pock-marked. As he drew closer, Greg could read the name stitched onto the front of the jacket: Harber. "What brings you up to Grand Butte DesMorts?"

Greg wanted to ask what he was talking about, but instead answered with a question. He was still but an observer. "Is there a problem, Officer Harber?"

"I reckon there is," Harber replied as his skin began to split and a grotesque form replaced that of the mild-mannered man. Greg fell away then, casting up a spell of protection and clamoring inside for his revolver. He felt pain now, no mere echo, like that in the fog. Desperate, he watched as this cabin, this horrific bloodletting, dissolved once more into that misty realm of shadow and gloom. But the pain was there waiting.

An echo no more, Greg Mitchell was ripped wide awake. He lay in a pool of his own blood, in a ditch between Sparrow Lane and the barren farmland. But no, it was no longer barren. Craning his neck, Greg could see that where there had once been only a ruined foundation, there now stood a rustic farmhouse, its paint peeling, shutters crooked. He could see his former mentor, Landon Connors, being drug up the porch steps by two men in suits, while a third stood before the farmhouse door. He was casting a spell, an intricate spiraling circle revolving at the end of his fingertips, strange letters assembling and rearranging, until suddenly they became locked and the green became golden. The man turned and addressed Connors.

"So you see, Landon," he said with a think British accent, "once again you are denied that which you have so diligently sought, and I shall reap the spoils of your pursuits."

"Oh, you'll get your just reward," Connors spat. "I'm sure of it."

The Brit laughed, and Greg Mitchell's vision swam. He could just make out the sight of them entering the house when he began to lose consciousness, his hands gripping the bullet wound in his gut. *I'm dying*, he thought, but then he felt a warmth filling him. There, above him, a shimmering light of what could only be described as infinite love shone down, and a voice whispered, "Not yet."

Chapter Seven

"*YOU*," LANDON CONNORS SPAT, gripping his cane with trembling rage. "What the bloody hell are you doing here?"

The British man chuckled. "Surely you didn't believe you were the only ones interested in this rather peculiar house, did you, Dr. Connors?"

Greg leaned closer, whispering. "You know who these guys are?"

"Yes," he replied heavily. "I know." Connors glowered at the well-dressed men and declared through bared teeth: "The Order of the Black Spire."

The bald British gentleman removed his wireframe glasses, casually took a silk cloth from his back pocket, and polished the lenses as he chuckled impishly, "You've been busy, old friend."

Connors stood his ground, watching with trepidation as the five suited men spread out, flanking he and Mitchell on all sides. "What do you know of this house?" the detective demanded.

The Briton—whom Connors knew to be Thorvald Haversham—finished his mundane task, resting the glasses back on his hooked nose. He grinned with great mirth, seemingly enjoying this moment to tremendous degree. "A fair bit more than you lot, obviously. Except, to be fair to the point, the *house* is not so much the thing as the land on which it rests."

Connors detected Greg's heated glare on him. "What do you mean?" the demonologist probed.

Haversham paced, hands clasped behind his back, stepping in the tall grass while Connors watched him warily. All around them, the Spire's agents remained stone stiff, their predatory gaze never lifting from Connors and his partner. "A convergence, my dear man. They exist in some form in all realities." He put a finger to his mouth, smirking. "Hmph, don't you love Christmas? I always found the holiday to be quite soothing. I have many fond memories of my childhood home on the lake. Of how my mother would sew a garland of popcorn to adorn the tree. Ha, yes. Quite pleasant." The man paused, lifting his face and hands to the heavens. "It would seem that God is not so different from my mother. The worlds are aligned in a garland, you see, held together on a string." He waved to the patch of grass where only a stone foundation rested, ancient with age. "This is merely where the needle punched through—the point through which the multiversal thread has passed. Our worlds hang by this thread, from this very point."

Connors seethed, but Greg chortled. "You're *nuts*."

Haversham brightened, amused. "Oh! More spirited than some of your other cohorts, Dr. Connors. I approve!" A dismissive wave of his hand to his nearest man, and Thorvald's gleeful demeanor became devilishly dark. "Kill him."

"Wait!" Connors reached out, but the faithful man immediately withdrew a 9mm and put a round in Mitchell's midsection.

The denim-clad hunter coughed in surprise, gaping at the expanding rose of red on his stomach.

"Greg!"

The Outrider paled and tipped sideways, eyes rolling into his head. Connors stepped toward him, but a tight fist intercepted from his right, socking him across the bearded jaw. Another strike from his left, driving into his stomach, expelled his breath. He wheezed, doubling over, and landed on all fours.

Snarling, he seethed at the Briton. "Damn you, Haversham!"

Once again, the man was downright cheery. "Oh, we're well beyond that, Landon, you and I? I daresay we will have the most marvelous conversations while we roast in the Pit, no?"

A sound like a foghorn split the tomb-quiet field, and a layer of mist rose from the tall grass, turning the world grey-white. Connors and the others looked around, dumbstruck, until Haversham retrieved a gold pocket watch from his suit coat and checked the time. "Well, well. Ahead of schedule."

The moan resounded again, and a dull green light pulsated from the soup. Haversham gestured to his men. "See to the body, will you?"

Three nodded, each grabbing an arm or leg of Greg Mitchell, carting his pale carcass away. Connors watched after them, tightening his hands into fists, curling the sodden earth between his fingers. Another friend lost in this war. Another friend he was unable to protect. Why did he persist in drafting others into his world, in training them? It was never enough. He was only ever condemning them to Mitchell's fate—to die alone.

"I'll kill you for this," he declared through his clenched jaw, but Haversham had long since moved on to other matters. The distinguished gentleman had his back to Connors, gazing in wonder at the shimmering shape before them. With each groan, the sight faded in and out like a mirage, slipping into this world and then the next—a farmhouse, altogether unremarkable and practically indistinguishable from hundreds Connors had passed in his journeys throughout the Midwest. Its windows were shuttered, its paint peeling. The wood was dark and warped, and the house sat at a slight angle on the stone foundation that had waited for its return.

No doubt, this was Mitchell's Hallowe'en House.

With one last burst of sickly green light, the house finally materialized and held its shape.

"Ah." Haversham clamped his watch shut and looked to his men. "Off to it, then." He snapped his fingers, and the men who'd struck Connors hooked him under each arm and dragged him behind the Spire's man. Connors sullenly looked behind him, watching as the other three crudely tossed Greg's body into a nearby ditch before dusting off their hands to march across the field and rejoin their fellows.

You deserved better, my friend…

Connors hung his head, allowing his captors to haul him like a sack of laundry. "Why, Thorvald? What does the Black Spire want with this house?"

"Can you imagine it, Doctor? A house that sits on the convergence of a thousand realities? It goes round and round, where it stops—no one knows! This is a doorway to infinite knowledge. Power! Think of what we could learn by visiting our dimensional neighbors—"

"And spread your heinous influence."

Haversham paused to smirk over his shoulder. "That, of course, goes without saying. The Spire reaches high—higher still, with this house in our possession. But locating it, at just the right moment when it entered into our phase, was something that has eluded our Order for over a century. Thanks to you, old friend," he mused, "we've finally succeeded."

The gentleman ascended the creaking farmhouse steps, stopping on the porch. Drawing his fingers in intricate patterns, Haversham began to emit a green light from his fingertips. With careful precision, the man wrote shimmering symbols on the air, and Connors boiled with fury. "What are you doing?"

"Marking this as our own. By binding it to my own astral energies, I ensure that we will not lose track of it again—no matter which dimension it escapes into." After a few moments, the wispy green letters solidified, locking into a golden-hued glow. "There. It is done." He lowered his arms, readjusting the cuffs on his sleeves. "So you see, Landon, once again you are denied that which you have so diligently sought, and I shall reap the spoils of your pursuits."

"Oh, you'll get your just reward," Connors spat. "I'm sure of it."

Haversham chortled as Mitchell's pallbearers returned. The Spire's men hauled Connors to the door, and the entire party crossed the threshold of the decrepit farmhouse. The Briton examined the dusty foyer, craning his head high to study the vaulted ceiling. Connors lifted his head, surveying the scene as well, but seeing nothing of note. Simple country furniture, out of date by nearly a hundred years. A Victrola on a stand by the staircase, a lamp—impossibly still illuminated, a chandelier swinging overhead, draped in cobwebs.

"Well," the man sniffed. "Charming."

"Urghk!" a startled cry shattered the terse silence of the moment. Connors, and all the others with him, turned in place to see one of the Spire agents at a rigid stance—a triangle of silver protruding from his sternum. The man gawked at the oozing wound, grunted with pain, then lowered.

Standing behind the agent, gripping the hilt of the silver short sword that had impaled him, was Greg Mitchell, scowling with contempt.

"Greg!" Connors cried.

Mitchell, somehow still alive, with not even a mark on his shirt to denote his fatal wound, retracted the blade, his victim collapsing with a heavy thud to the hardwood floor. Haversham stepped back, outraged. "Kill him!"

Greg swung out with his sword, severing a gunman's hand at the wrist. Another man fired twice—*pop-pop*—but Mitchell spun out of the way, dropping low and slicing through the attacker's knees. Crippled, the gunman screamed and fell onto his face.

"That's a good showing, lad!" Connors cheered.

The twirling swordsman gripped something in his other hand and tossed it. "Drop something, old chum?"

Connors saw his cane flying for him, then gathered his strength and stood, elbowing one of his captors in the stomach. The man released his arm, and the occult detective outstretched his hand, securing the cane in mid-flight. Immediately, he turned it on his other foe, clocking him across the bridge of the nose, then bringing it down in a violent swing on the first man, who was still doubled over regaining his breath.

Mitchell lunged for the fourth agent, running him through the stomach, before spinning to press his back to Connors. The Outrider was huffing, invigorated with life, and Connors marveled at the sight, "How?"

Greg grimaced. "Tell you later."

Together, the partners turned on Haversham, who stepped back, tentative hands held before his face. "Now, gentlemen—"

Suddenly, the front door to the farmhouse slammed shut with a reverberating thundercrack. Connors and his companion whirled on their feet and glimpsed the sight outside the front windows. Through the sheer drapes they saw not the field in Alix, but a spinning cyclone of oily, alien color. The house pitched and groaned, its eaves buckling with strain. The ground rattled, the furniture tremoring in place.

All the while, Haversham laughed uproariously. "Anyone fancy a trip through the multiverse?"

Connors and Mitchell shared a worried look.

"Well…" Greg sighed, his broad shoulders sagging, "crap."

Chapter Eight

"Y'ALL RECKON YOU COULD quiet down now? You done gone and woke Mama, and she 'nd I don't take kindly to disturbances, particularly of the violent kind."

Connors, Mitchell, and Haversham turned to see a vision descending the rickety stairs. A shaft of gold and purple light followed her, emanating from a stained glass ocular window at the top of the landing. Her hair was a soft ginger, spilling across milky white shoulders. Her white cotton peasant dress did little to disguise her majestic form.

"Madam," Haversham began, bowing as she approached, "please forgive our trespass. I, for one, was unaware this abode was occupied, let alone by someone of such elegance." The Englishman reached out and took her hand, lowering himself to deliver a gentle kiss on its alabaster dorsum.

Connors removed his hat, offering the woman a nod of his head, while Greg held out his hand to shake hers. Her delicate fingers wrapped around the demonologist's calloused hand, and he felt his heart quicken. He was amazed by the softness of her skin, of how fragile she felt, but at the same time, Greg could feel an inner strength, an almost preternatural energy, that shivered him to the core.

"Charmed," she said, her voice melodic and hypnotizing. Her eyes, a vibrant green with flecks of orange scattered about the iris, flickered, capturing the inky, unnatural sky that now surrounded the farmhouse.

"Miss...?" Connors began. He paused for her to fill in the blank.

"Buckland," she replied. "Raylene Buckland."

"Miss Buckland," Connors continued. He took her hand gently, rolling his thumb on the middle knuckle and sliding his finger along her wrist as he released her. "It is my utmost pleasure to make your acquaintance. I do apologize for this unsightly scene before you. We mean no disrespect to you or your...mother."

"It's true, ma'am," Mitchell added. "We had no idea the house was lived in." He looked to the bodies littering the front room. The men were dead or dying, a swath of blood sprayed across the rough, hardwood floors and the threadbare ornamental rug beneath their feet. "We believed this place to be...untethered."

"Untethered," she said, a demure laugh and smile escaping her lips. "What a delightful word for it." She stepped toward him, her back to Haversham and Connors. She raised an arm, slowly, deliberately, and with her left hand, gently caressed Mitchell's cheek. "We're beyond the pale, darlin'." She leaned in close, her cheek brushing his, and whispered into his ear. "Some folks call it the *Otherside* or the *In-Between*, but there ain't no right word for what it really is, if you follow my line of thinkin'."

"I-I think I do, miss," Greg responded.

"Yeah, I just bet you do." She turned, swiftly, pirouetting with a dancer's grace, to face Haversham and Connors. "And you all, well I reckon the two of you think you've got it all sussed and figured, but ya don't know the half of it if'n you were to take both of your thinkin' and mash it into clay and mold it into somethin' discernible." She walked between them and placed a hand on each of their chests. "Y'all are flip sides of the same buffalo nickel and worth half as much, or so Mama says."

"I would be remiss if I didn't offer up my regrets to your mother, in person, Miss Buckland," Haversham said. His eyes darted toward

Connors who detected his adversary's wry sneer. "I am dismayed by our shameful display and would love the opportunity to convey my deepest respects and apologies to her."

"I just bet you would, silver tongue," Buckland replied. She danced away from them, bare foot on hardwood. She seemed to glide across the floor. She stopped at the window overlooking the side yard and drew back the curtain. Her skin took on a crimson cast, reflections from an exploding morass of celestial fireworks in the otherwise expansive sea of greens, purples, violets, and black. "Isn't it just the purtiest thing y'all e'er seen?" She closed the curtain and spun about, the light behind her all but erasing her peasant dress. "This is my favorite part, when we're adrift." She smiled, coyly. "When we're *untethered*." She winked at Greg.

"How long have you been...?" Connors began. He stepped toward her as he began to speak, but the young woman raised her hand and he froze in place and found himself unable to continue.

"Untethered? Adrift? Dislodged from the prime material?" she snapped. Her brow became furrowed. Her face darkened. Haversham began to sweat. His fingers began to quickly manipulate the telluric fabric of extradimensional magics that surrounded all living things, but with the flick of her wrist, he was tossed aside, hurtling backward to crash into the stair banister. Greg held up both hands in defense.

"Miss Buckland," he said, taking a step back, "we mean you no harm."

"Is that so, Greg Mitchell?" she said, her gentle voice now coarse and seething. "I know your kin." She walked toward him, impossibly fast. "I smell ya, all y'all, back to the olden days. Hell's fire, boy, I can smell ya all the way back to them thar caves when y'all were spinnin' haint yarns 'round the campfire." She poked her finger into Mitchell's chest. "Y'all been wrong-sided from day one, I'm here to tell ya, and I'm about to take y'all to school, or rather, I would be," she relaxed, her demeanor returning to its less volatile state, "if'n Mama would let me."

Haversham stirred from his place on the floor as Connors stumbled forward, suddenly loosed from her sorcerous grip. Haversham rose, holding his arm awkwardly as he took his place beside Connors. Greg spun and back-stepped till he too was standing with them.

"What's that, Mama?" Miss Buckland said. The three men heard nothing. "Yes, Mama," she said again, as if talking to the very air itself. She smoothed out the ruffles in her dress and stood tall before them. "I am to invite one of you to an audience with Mama," she said, as properly as she could muster. The three men looked to one another. Haversham scowled at his rivals and then took a step forward, still nursing his left arm.

"I believe, madam," the Englishman began, "I am the most suitable to make your mother's acquaintance." He gripped his elbow and a warm glow spread over him. He then moved the limb freely, testing its mobility, confident that he'd healed himself satisfactorily.

"Thorvald Wallace Haversham, Magus 9=2," Miss Buckland said. She approached him, and despite her earlier display of power, Haversham, to his credit, didn't flinch. "You're used to bein' the top dog, now aren't ya? Big shot at the head of the table of your little black mountain, surrounded by snakes, but I reckon you're more venomous than the lot of them by far." She circled him, running her hand across his chest, shoulder, back. From behind, she leaned in and whispered, "Oh, Mama would like you, I think. That tongue of yours would wag itself silly, and she'd rightly swoon from your charms, but..." She moved away from him and turned her attention to Connors.

"...Landon Ashton Connors. My, oh, my, what a long drink of water you are." She flung her arms around his head and kissed him wetly on the mouth, which he reciprocated. "You put on airs a bit. Nothing quite as ostentatious as Mr. Haversham here, but you're a showman, yes indeed." Her hands slid down his chest and she gripped his pants at the waist and pulled him into her forcibly. "You're awfully pretty for a man. Mama would love those eyes of yours, but then..." She slid away from the occult detective, spinning so that her dress fanned out.

"...Greg," she said, reaching out and taking him by the hand. "Yeah, Greg here is practically family, aren't you, boy." She led him away from the others, to the base of the stairs. "Mama will want to jaw with you a spell, I think."

Greg looked to Connors, somewhat wide-eyed, who nodded to his former student. He made a slight hand gesture, a private signal between them. It meant, be careful, be on guard. Greg nodded back and followed Raylene Buckland up the creaking stairs.

Chapter Nine

GREG ASCENDED TO THE FARMHOUSE'S second story with the ethereal Raylene Buckland as his guide. They wound around the first flight, rounding a corner so that Greg could no longer see Connors and Haversham below. He felt horribly alone and unprepared for whatever this stranger had waiting for him—she and her "Mama". Only moments ago, he'd been dead, or close to it, spared by divine intervention that he hadn't had a second's rest to process. God had saved him, but why?

All Greg could do was follow the winding staircase, climbing further into darkness. The hallways became blacker, with only the billowing alien colours outside to guide his steps. Before long, he lost track of himself—of the house entirely—as it seemed they had passed through boards and nails and now glided along the stars. Or, he supposed, the spaces *between* the stars.

"What is this place?" he whispered in reverence, the cyclone of multiversal reality blurring past him. Every so often he caught glimpses into other realms, other worlds. Saw other lives that he'd never lead. MAlice was there, too, with a family they'd never share.

His guide tittered with madness. "A house, I reckon. Might fine, one, no doubt. Lasted this long, did'nit?"

"How long, exactly?"

"Who can say? We ousside a Time, lookin' in." She gestured to the storm of realities that swept around them like a hurricane. "See any ya like?"

"Why does…Mama want to see me, Miss Buckland?"

"Best *she* tell ye."

Greg firmed his mouth, unable to take his eyes off the sashaying form of his alluring host. In the twisting maelstrom of witch-light, her every bend and curve was a temptation to his animal urges. Her slip was threadbare and showed her fine and supple form.

Raylene merely glanced over her shoulder, smiling at him, peering through his holy veneer to the sinful man that fought for control inside. "Oh, I see you very well, Greg Mitchell. You *have* found somethin' ya like, eh?"

He blushed and looked away, scolding himself for his moment of weakness.

She reached out, took hold of the edge of his jacket, and gave it a soft tug, leading him on like a puppy—or, more accurately, a lamb to slaughter. "Right this way."

Up ahead, at the peak of a mountain of night, rested an unremarkable door. As he neared it, the clop-clopping of his boots on wooden steps returned. The house materialized around them, their long passage through the ages behind. Raylene offered a sly wink, then turned the knob, giving the door a push open.

"Mama," she announced, her enchanting green eyes continuing to luridly roam over Greg's body. "We got comp'ny."

The door creaked wider, revealing a darkened bedroom. The blinds on the window hung crooked and were nearly entirely shut, as the sickening psychedelic colours outside permeated the gloom, cutting like shifting lasers across the expanse of the room. In the low light, Greg spotted a globular shape on a lopsided bed. The sheets were strewn, as though the occupant rarely left—and the occupant in question was a morbidly rotund woman, dressed in the same sort of simple peasant slip as Raylene. She was a mound of cellulite, reclined against a trio of floppy pillows so that her head was barely visible above her girth. The bedridden woman cooled her sweaty face with a fan, and Greg noted it *was* awfully humid inside her lair.

He cleared his throat, and when neither Raylene nor the other woman spoke, he finally said, "Mama?"

The woman sized him up, her shadowed features only highlighted sporadically by the shifting cosmic glow outside the house.

"I brung him, just like you wanted," Raylene told the lump on the bed.

"Fetch me some lemonade, Raylene, hun," Mama commanded in a slow, phlegmy drawl devoid of any sort of compassion. "And shet the door behind ya. We need us some privacy."

"Yes, Mama." Raylene did as instructed, hands clasped before her, head bowed in faithful humility. She offered Greg a look he couldn't quite define—as though he were about to share in a secret only she'd been previously privy to. There was excitement in her gaze but apprehension as well. Greg watched her leave, then returned his anxious glance to Mama.

The woman did not immediately speak, rather allowing an uncomfortable silence to swell, filling every shadowed nook of the sweltering bedroom. In an especially bright flare of rainbow-coloured light, Greg allowed himself a moment's distraction to study as much detail of the room as he could before it dimmed to shade once more. He saw a bedroom not so different than those of most old women, he supposed. Old knick-knacks adorned a dresser alongside an open jewelry box with unremarkable necklaces draped over the edges. He saw black-and-white portraits lining the shelves and the wall but could not quite discern the faces in the passing light. Altogether, an ordinary room—except for the monster that dwelled within it.

"You wanted to see me, ma'am?" he probed, still keeping his voice light, praying his thumping heart would not create too noticeable a quaver in his speech.

She snorted and sneered through yellowed, tiny, crooked teeth. "Did you want a lemonade, hun? I done forgot to ask Raylene for you—"

He huffed, frustrated. "I'm fine." Braving, he demanded, "Who are you?"

"Right to it, then." She fanned herself, craning her lumpy neck this way and that to dry the sweat there. "Oh, alright. I s'pose it's too hot for small talk anyhow." She leveled a withering eye on him. "Still, seein' as you'uns are in *my* house, I reserve the right to ask the questions 'round here." Mama waved to the eddies that stretched around the house like taffy made of polychromatic light. "I been in this ole house a long, long time. I seen a lot through my bedroom winda."

"If I may ask…*Mama*," Greg began delicately, "How did you come by this house?"

"Been in my family for ages, boy," she laughed, and when she did so, the bed creaked beneath her trembling weight. "Ever since my kin called to the Master of the House, as it were." She chortled again, a wet, nasally sound. "But that ain't why I wanted to speak with you'un. At least, not entirely. See, my time is drawing to an end. Gettin' bout ready to step outside there—" she inclined her round head towards the dancing lights. "—and soon it'll be Raylene who runs the place. But Raylene gon need a man. She'll need youngins one day, herself. To carry on, ya understand."

Greg nearly choked. "Wait, what?"

"Oh, I know you been eyeing her. And she, *you*, don't you worry none. See, we seen you outside our winda from time to time. You been traipsing through our backyard for years."

He frowned. "What do you mean?"

She groaned and laughed. "Don't you play at that now. We seen you, when you slip outta yer skin like a serpent. Your soul slithers about— well, now, boy, where'd you think it gone to, but out here? With us, in the *In-Between*." She reached out with a doughy toe, poking at his leg. "And here you gone passin' by our front porch time and again, and never stopping to say 'hello'."

Greg considered this. "I'm sorry if I was…rude. I didn't know."

Her laughter died down, and her gaze settled to an intense beady-eyed stare. Even in the darkness, tiny pinpricks of light shone from her eyes. "No, son, you didn't. I 'spect there's much you don't know about the way a'things." A thoughtful pause. "You a holy man, is it?"

"No," he said with some shame, knowing he tried to be, but often failed.

"Oh, yes you is. When the wind's still, I hears yer prayers. Cryin' out to God to f'rgive you, to guide you." Once more with that fat toe—the toenail painted red, he noted—she caressed his thigh. "Wanna know a secret? I can show you where your God lives, too. But he ain't much to look at these days. Just an old, blind fool, fumbling in the dark for a hand."

Greg took a step back, smirking. This wasn't the first demon to attempt to shake his faith. "Liar."

She saw his casual defiance and winked, playfully admitting her deception. "Maybe I am. Maybe I ain't. Guess we'll all see in the end, won't we, hun?"

"Guess so, Mama." Greg bowed with respect. "Thank you for seeing me, but I'm afraid I'll have to turn down your offer."

Greg pivoted on his heel, reaching for the door, before Mama sang back after him. "Your Daddy was a holy man, too."

His hand froze, fingers barely brushing the polished handle. She was baiting him, he knew, and he also knew what Landon would say. He'd caution him not to engage the she-devil any further. There was still so much they didn't know about this house—or about the Mama who ran it—and it would be foolish to play into her obvious manipulations.

But he faced her anyway. "What about my Dad?"

"Got yer attention, did it? Yessir, he came 'round these parts. Thirty year ago, was it? Such a sensitive young man, like you are now. This house, see, it *called* to him too. So, Billy and I went for a spin. I showed him the worlds. Let him see the past, his future—even took him beyond it all where there's only truth and terror. Oh, yes, he saw *so many* things.

Even introduced him to the Master of the House. They had a good talk that day," she finished with a bright laugh.

Greg clenched his jaw, thinking of his father. Of the fear the man had of this house. "I'm not him," he declared.

"You will lie among dead flowers," the woman repeated the warning from Greg's vision. "Dirt shall be your just reward. Wanna see?"

She nodded to the window without guile or satisfaction. Greg thought to shut his eyes, knowing he was walking headlong into madness…but could not stop. Glaring at her in disgust, he crossed the room and peeked through the blinds. Gone were the alien lights—now there was only a humble cabin.

A cabin in the woods.

He recognized it. It was one of the safehouses that Landon offered to Outriders passing through on hunts. Greg had stayed there, himself, on occasion during his apprenticeship to Connors. But this wasn't a vision of those heady days of spellweaving, rather a glimpse into the future. Into *his* future.

Greg saw himself, splayed out on the hard wood floor, still and drenched in blood. *Mine?* Kneeling over him, Landon Connors held a sharpened knife in his steady hand and sawed at Greg's neck, severing his head—

Greg Mitchell backed away, instinctively clutching his throat, tears stinging his eyes.

"Just dirt," Mama called behind him. "All that work you done for God, and all you get for it is an unmarked grave?"

Greg touched his damp forehead, controlling his fevered breathing. What was Landon doing to him? And *why?*

Mama crooned, "But that don't gotta be the way. That's only one path for you—but out here, with us, you can choose any you want. That cabin, that really what you want for your life? I'm offering you *forever*, hun."

Greg felt bile rising in the back of his mouth but swallowed it down. He only needed a moment to brace himself against the wall, to dislodge the fear that clamored to grow up like weeds in his heart to pull him down in despair. "Is this… Is this what you showed my father?"

"Not the cabin, no, but every man's got his own cabin, don't you think? I showed your Daddy his. That hospital bed, hooked up to machines, relatives fightin' over what he leaves behind. He'll die screaming in the dark, boy, and no one will be there with him in the final hour. He'll die afraid, and then we'll see who was right about God."

Greg trembled, wanting to return home. To be with his dad, to keep him from passing alone. He moved for the door with newfound determination but flinched when it opened and Raylene entered with a tray bearing a pitcher of lemonade and two empty glasses. She looked startled by Greg's march, then tittered, uneasy. "Got your lemonade, Mama."

"Pour me some, hun. Buildin' up a might thirst from all this jawin'."

Raylene did, eyeing Greg carefully. "Did you tell him yet, Mama?"

"We was right there, sugar. You made it in time for the best part."

With tears blurring his vision, Greg snarled in anger, "I'm through listening to you."

"Oh, not yet! We ain't made it to the whole truth, yet, son. There's still one more thing left to say. Y'see, your Daddy, Billy, was in such a tizzy when I showed him his end, that I had to *comfort* him, ya understand."

Greg's gut soured. "Liar," he spat again, though with less resolve than before.

"No lies *this* time." She spread her hands across the mildewed sheets. "It was right here, I invited him in. Oh, he blubbered like a baby, on account of your mother—"

Greg balled up his fists and charged the woman. "Shut up!"

"—but he didn't put up much of a fight. See, I was much prettier back in them days." She cast a pudgy hand, sweeping it across the mantle, drawing his attention to the framed photos he'd seen earlier. Indeed, within the frames he saw images of a ravishing beauty with the same gold-flecked green eyes as Raylene, the same unruly firebrand hair.

"After we was through, though," she began, putting on an air of sadness, though Greg understood it was meant to mock him, "he was filled with such *guilt*. He left here, left my Master," she nodded to Raylene, still pouring the lemonade, "but he left something behind."

At this, Raylene looked up at Greg, shy, but grinning wide.

"My God," he gasped.

"So, you see," Mama began, "we like kin. You're home, boy. This house is *yours*."

Chapter Ten

CONNORS WAS PACING, the dull ache of his ruined knee his constant companion. He had opened the curtains, all of them, so that the twisting soup of cosmic, ethereal madness was with them as an ever-present reminder that they were not in Kansas anymore. Well, *Arkansas*, anyway. Haversham had remained quiet, solemnly staring out across the great expanse of celestial ataxia with a grim look of...*satisfaction*? It was hard to say. Connors mulled it over, curious as to the depth of his adversary's knowledge of this place, but unwilling to scratch that itch. His concern for his former student's journey into the aerie of the farmhouse was more pressing. When Haversham finally broke the silence, Connors was almost thankful.

"I knew your father well," the Englishman said suddenly, but with the same cool and collected demeanor that he bore like a fine tempered shield. "Perhaps far better than you realize." The black magician never looked away from the window. "He was a... remarkable man, your father. Erudite and insightful, to a fault. Though we were on opposing sides in our quest, we shared a common bond, a fraternal engagement, if you will. He is missed."

"Missed?" Connors lit a cigarette. "You got some nerve, Haversham." He walked up behind the Englishman's left shoulder. The

occult detective could see their reflections against the window, could see their furrowed brows and steely eyes. Were they really so different? Their mutual distaste for one another was revelatory. Was this the sort of bond he was speaking of? He suddenly reflected on their paths, wondering where they'd be a decade from now, two. Would they see each other as old friends, despite their differing philosophies and scores of battles waged in the occult arena? No, Connors mused. He couldn't see it.

"My father died horribly," Connors continued. "I am maimed for life." He pressed his cane, the twisted one that had been first Crowley's, then his father's, hard into Haversham's back, forcing the man to stagger forward. He spun about, fists clenched. "So when you tell me you miss my father, I can't help but think that, were it not for you and the Order, he'd still be here with us."

"No one told you to venture south, boy," Haversham snapped. "To traverse those icy mountains and dare the madness that lies within those frigid caves of chaos. A fool's errand. Your father should have known better, and if not, then he should have been better prepared to face the darkness that made that hallowed place its abode."

"You bastard," Connors sneered.

"Bastard? Perhaps, whelp, but if you poke a shoggoth, what do you bloody expect?" Haversham pushed past him, walking toward the stair leading to the upper story of the untethered farmhouse. "And here we are, trapped in this place, together, you and I. Do you smell it? Is this place really so different than the cave where your father met his fate?" His eyes drifted upward.

"Now that you mention it," Connors said. He took a long drag off his cigarette, then dropped it to the floor, snubbing it out with his heel. "Humor me." Connors slid out of his trench coat and rifled through its pockets. With a grimace, he reached down, grabbed the corner of the area rug, and flung it back, dragging it to the far side of the room.

"What are you up to, mate?" Haversham asked.

Connors ignored the man as he took the chalk he'd retrieved from his coat and began to craft an intricately drawn circle on the floor. It was roughly nine feet in diameter, with two inner rings. In the first ring Connors inscribed an Enochian orison, while in the second he strategically placed astrological and elemental sigils meant to unlock certain portals in the interwoven multiverse. Then in the center, the occult detective constructed a web of connecting lines, infusing the symbols with arcane energies through the power of reciprocity.

"What did I bloody say about poking shoggoths, lad?" Haversham said. He knelt down, closely examining the detective's work. "You're mad, like your father."

"That's right, Haversham," Connors said. He was sweating profusely. He tipped his worn fedora back on his forehead, letting his auburn locks spill down across his face. He looked up through his tousled hair and smiled. "You hit on it, you old devil," Connors continued. "The smell of this place, the timbre of it. And you know more than you've been letting on. It's no wonder the Order of the Black Spire wanted to make this place their own." Connors sat cross-legged in the center of the circle and began to manipulate magical currents with his fingertips, tracing kennings in the air that reverberated through the delicate construct of all creation. "I can feel it now, its presence, and the presence of its sleeping master."

"Don't say it, boy," Haversham warned.

"Why not?" Connors snapped. "Its servants already tipped their hand. Mitchell and I crossed Maelfix's path on the road to this place." He held up his right hand, commanding silence. Raising his forefinger, he drew it in close to his face, brushing his lips, while his left palm came to rest over his heart, then, making a fist, he raised his left defiantly, fingers fanning out.

"Bloody hell," Haversham muttered. He snatched up Connors' discarded chalk and began to hurriedly construct a circle of protection. Just as he closed the magical sphere there was a sound, like a distant sonic boom, and the house shook. Looking outside, Haversham saw the colours intensify, to pulse with a shimmering ferocity as the purpling hues gave way to a sweltering and consuming inky blackness.

"ISA YA! ISA YA! RI EGA! RI EGA! BI ESHA BI ESHA! XIYILQA! XIYILQA! DUPPIRA ATLAKA ISA YA U RI EGA!" Connors cried out. He raised his right hand to emulate his left. Slowly he brought the forefingers and thumbs together.

"Foolish, lad," Haversham muttered. "Damned foolish."

"LIMUTTIKUNU KIMA QUTRI LITILLI SHAMI YE! INA ZUMRI YA ISA YA! INA ZUMRI YA RI EGA! INA ZUMRI YA BI ESHA! INA ZUMRI YA XIYILQA! INA ZUMRI YA DUPPIRA! INA ZUMRI YA ATLAKA! INA ZUMRI YA LA TATARA!" Connors bent forward and slammed both palms onto the floor, and there was a great whooshing sound that expanded outward from his touch. Haversham was staggered. Fighting to keep his balance, the Brit clawed both hands, right above left, and conjured a ball of eldritch energy, holding it in check, sweat cascading down his furrowed brow.

"INA ZUMRI YA LA TETIXXI YE!" Connors whispered. Face down, he inhaled slowly and began to raise his shoulders, loose, arms hanging limp. "INA ZUMRI YA LA TAQARRUBA! INA ZUMRI YA LA TASANIQA! NI YISH SHAMMASH KABTU LU TAMATUNU!" Returning to his cross-legged position, Connors began to rise, levitating off the hardwood floor. "NI YISH ENKI BEL GIMRI LU TAMATUNU!" he called out, his voice hoarse and strained. "NI YISH MARDUK MASHMASH ILANI LU TAMATUNU!" the occult detective muttered, almost unintelligently. "NI YISH GISHBAR QAMIKUNU LU TAMATUNU!"

"Drormagondulac," Haversham said, his eyes gone white.

"INA ZUMRI YA LU YU TAPPARRASAMA!"

Connors' voice crackled like fire. He thrust his arms wide as his feet lowered and found purchase on the floor below. He slid into some sort of combative stance while behind him, Haversham did the same. The Englishman maintained the magical sphere between his palms, drawing his arms back and to the right, hands shaking.

Overhead, a shadow passed, like the fluttering of wings. Something tumbled from a nearby shelf, a curio box, dusty and old. From it spilled the hilt of an athame, its blade broken and rust-pitted, but it was quickly obscured by a fetid mist that began seeping in from under the door and from cracks in the window. It billowed around the magicians' protective circles, unable to penetrate them.

"The worm turns," Haversham said.

Odd shapes moved in the fog, shadowy figures, horned and hooved but with the bodies of men. Worse was the cruel, but distant laughter, and somewhere a cock crowed. Then it was gone as suddenly as it had come, and the room was empty as before.

"Show yourself!" Connors screamed.

"Shh," a voice responded from the door. It opened slowly, and the silhouette of a woman stood framed in the doorway. Behind her, a candlelit library stretched as far as they could see. With a wave of her hand, the door closed, and she stepped forward.

"Dr. Connors, I presume," the woman said as she closed the distance between her and the occult detective's circle of protection. "We've not had the pleasure."

"Baltruska," Haversham said. His concentration broken, the ball of eldritch energy he held dissipated. His eyes met hers, and with a flick of the wrist his circle was shattered, and he crumbled to the floor, unmoving.

Connors stood his ground, as the woman's gaze rose to the ceiling above them. She smiled as the occult detective heard his former student cry out. Something wet touched his cheek. He brushed it away and discovered it to be dripping blood from overhead.

"Greg," Connors muttered.

"Let's not worry about him, little mage," the woman said. Her hand caressed the invisible barrier between them. "Let's talk about us."

Chapter Eleven

HIS FATHER ALWAYS CRIED after beating him.

TWHAP!

The length of barbed hemp had bitten into Greg's back, down there in the basement back in Mountain Rest, and the thirteen-year-old boy did not let out a scream or shout. Ahead of him, at the center of his intense focus, the portrait of Christ and the Sacred Heart. In those excruciating sessions, Greg would focus on the eyes of his Lord and recall the Savior's final words: *Forgive them, for they know not what they do.*

Behind him, his father would lash out again, snarling in rage, making demands against the universe that his son would not be involved with the endless conflict between Light and Dark. In those dark moments, there in the dank, stone basement, Bill Mitchell fought against Fate—or so he had believed—as though with enough lashes he might ruin his son from being fit for *either* side and somehow safe.

But he had always cried when he was finished.

Late into the night, while Greg sat on his bed upstairs, as his mother gently applied salve to his wounds, he had heard his father's anguished wails coming from the other room. All these years later, above the pain and the terror—even beyond the scars he still bore on his back—Greg Mitchell thought of his father's sobbing most of all.

Looking at the morbid creature in the bed before him, Greg thought he finally understood when those tears had first begun to flow.

"The House needs a watcher," Mama was saying, as her daughter—Greg's own half-sister—poured her another glass of lemonade. "We ride the rifts, turning our face to the worlds. Always spinnin', always visitin'."

"But *why*?" Greg rasped, desperate to know, to understand this maddening, hideous place.

"We the ferrymen." Mama paused long enough to gulp her drink, dribbling some on her flabby breasts.

"Of souls? A psychopomp?"

"Not of souls—of *others*," Raylene finished for her mother. "Those ousside'a Time. Those looking to get in."

After swallowing, Mama finished, "We spin and we spin, opening up our home to many boarders." She gestured to the darkened ceiling, and, there, Greg saw the boards ripple and bow with movement from above. In the black cracks, many eyes blinked back at him, as whispers and snickers met his ears. Dark, hairy arms and sharpened claws peeked out from between the slats. "We spin and we spin," Mama sang again, "offering them safe passage to the worlds."

"We the halfway house of hell," Raylene tittered, quite mad.

Greg worried his brow, struggling with the ramifications of such an operation. "You ferry demons… You *sow evil* across the multiverse."

"Evil's already there, hun," Mama said. "We just bringing more hands in to work the fields, thass'all."

Raylene frowned. "But Mama's taken ill. She ain't got too long left…and I cain't run this house on my own." Facing the Outrider with a sincerity he'd not yet seen in her, the sultry temptress begged, "Stay with me."

He shook his head. "This is madness."

Mama snickered into her glass. "Better'n the alternative, son. Wouldn't you say? You think you can trust that friend a'yours downstairs? The purty man? He's gon cut your head clean off!"

Greg's stomach churned. "I don't believe that. You're lying—"

She rolled her eyes dramatically. "Oh, we're back to this agin? I done told you, boy. I'm just showing you the way of things and givin' you another path."

Raylene set down her tray long enough to run her hands along her wide, inviting hips. "I know you like me. It won't be bad—I promise."

Overhead, the unseen devils drew in for a look, slobbering over the seductress and their potential blasphemous union. Greg heard their snorts, their purrs, and his soul shook. Outside, the lights danced drunkenly, and in here, this fat woman was trying to whore his own half-sister to him.

His father had been right. This place was surely hell.

From some distant memory, he heard the whip snap against his soft flesh and his father's weeping that always followed.

"You broke him," Greg said in a whisper.

Mama merely sipped her lemonade, while Raylene hung her head, rejected. She retrieved her tray, a slave to the matron of this unholy house.

"He never forgave himself for what happened here," Greg continued, glaring at the devils in the dark. They shrank back from him, hissing. "After that, he only ever saw God as a disapproving and demanding Master. He was forever in fear of Him." Shaking his head, he spat at the bedridden crone, "But what you meant for evil, God turned to good. See, I *found* God in that basement—as He really is. He is patient, and merciful, and, no, He doesn't promise to always stop the bad things that happen to you—but He *will be* there with you in it, and you will be made stronger for it."

Mama gestured for Raylene, then returned her empty glass to the tray that she offered.

Upon seeing he was ignored, Greg stepped closer to the rotund shape on the bed. "I died on your front porch, *Mama*, but He brought me back. To end you."

At last, she chortled. "Oh, is that so, holy man?"

A multitude of growls rattled the rafters as the house shuddered around them. Greg braced himself against the bed post for balance, and the tray in Raylene's hand slipped to the floorboards, where it crashed.

Mama only laughed, her cackles rising. "Don't preach at me, fool boy. Your end is written—whatever you think you'll accomplish here, you will die in that cabin!"

"Maybe I will, maybe I won't," he shouted over the groaning farmhouse and its hellish boarders. "But I won't abandon those who need my help, or my friends—*or* my God!" Standing taller, shouting down the fat woman, he declared, "I *will not stop* until He chooses to take me home! Do you hear me?!" He threw back his jacket and drew his silver short sword. "Die, harlot of Satan!"

Greg leapt onto the bed, ready to slay the creature that had devastated his family, when Raylene hollered out in shrill fright. "Mama!"

The shapely beauty extended her hands, hooking her fingers as claws, and an invisible force slammed into Mitchell from the side, casting him across the room and against the dresser. He landed hard on his ribs, hearing a crack, knocking aside Mama's framed pictures and porcelain collectibles. He landed on the floor with an "oof", decorated by a shower of junk, and immediately noticed his hands were empty.

The sword lay some distance away, just out of reach.

Raylene stood before the disabled blob, hands raised, as the alien lights outside the windows writhed in expectation and the horned, hooved shapes in shadows crawled and prowled about the floor, nearing him. The woman's eyes glowed white. "You won't hurt her! I'll kill you first!"

Greg looked up to his half-sister, pleading. "You don't have to protect her. You don't have to be a slave to this blasted house! You have a choice, too—leave here with me!"

Raylene's fury faltered, while Mama blurted from the bed, "Where you think she'd *go*, boy? With you? Go meet her Pappy afore he faces his final judgment?"

Greg rose, unarmed, mindful of the hooved shapes that clomped and stamped around his discarded blade. He ignored them, offering his hand to the white-eyed witch. "Come with me," he repeated softly, only to her, heedless of the devils that crowded them.

Raylene blinked in confusion, the gold-speckled green of her irises restored. She looked to the proffered hand with uncertainty.

"Enough a'this!" Mama huffed from the bed, raising her plump arms high. "Eat 'em *both*!"

Raylene gaped at the crone, wide-eyed with terror. "M-Mama?"

The horned figures rose taller, flexing their broad shoulders, sneering down with gleaming white lion's fangs that shone against the dark. Raylene slowly wheeled about as the shapes moved in, their talons twitching.

"Down!" Greg clasped his sister's hand and yanked her out of the way, then released her even as he clambered towards his blade on his knees. He scooped up the handle, then swung upwards, slashing through a living shadow. The goatish devil squalled in agony, its midsection fizzling into vapor. Black gunk splashed to the wooden floor, splattering against Greg's jeans. The demons blinked at their disemboweled kin, then to one another, before charging at the Outrider.

Baring his teeth, he rose and twirled, cutting through the air in a deadly arc. Horns and heads faded to charcoal wisps that filled the room with the smell of brimstone, rivers of inky sludge spilling from the orifices to run along the boards. Greg hacked again and again, ducking their claws, sidestepping their lunges. He sensed holy fire welling inside him and remembered his purpose. All the torments he'd endured, all the shame, the rage—none of that meant anything. *This* was who he was. And, if what the witch had showed him out in the cabin was true, he would die fighting.

He supposed he couldn't ask for anything more.

Lost in reflection, Greg faltered in his step, opening up his defenses for a pair of brawny, smoky arms to encircle him from behind. He let out a sharp, startled cry, hefted off his feet, then watched one of the beast's companions racing in for the kill. Mitchell dislodged his spirit, allowing his captor to clutch his empty shell, while his soul leapt ahead. Incorporeal, he tangled with the onrushing devil, the two of them wrestling inches off the ground, otherworldly light clashing with a fog of darkness. They wove in and out of one another, battling for supremacy, until a shimmering ripple of green-white light spiraled from across the room. The torrent of power crashed against the fell creature who held Greg's husk, reducing the demon's form to exploding ichor.

Greg's soul gasped, immediately reeled back into his body. Suddenly bathed in black, the rejoined Mitchell landed on the floor, spitting out the excess from his mouth. He looked to his salvation, Raylene Buckland, who stormed forward, eyes white fire, hands raised.

She screeched like a banshee and cast an unseen force that swept across the floor in a tidal wave of supernatural might. The remaining demons howled, caught in the radius, detonating and painting the walls and flooring in clumpy slime, absolutely soaking the room. Greg, too, was caught in the blast, and tumbled end over end, rebounding off the wall in a daze. He shook loose his vertigo, and when he looked up, he saw a delicate moon-white hand held out for him.

Raylene smiled down, not the same alluring sneer from earlier, but an honest—and somewhat frightened—grin. He accepted her aid and was helped to his feet. Still clutching one another's hands, the half-siblings faced the dreadful Mama.

The fat creature practically bounced on her knees, wobbling around in her squalor. In a fit of rage, she reached for the empty lemonade glass on the nightstand and flung it at the duo. They easily dodged it, and it popped against the wall—but when Greg turned back to the hateful crone, he balked in surprise to see Mama airborne, flying straight for him.

Without thinking, he knelt and brought up his blade. Still screaming, Mama landed on its bloodied, pointed tip, her immense gut swallowing the short sword as she slid down to the hilt. Spitted on its silver edge, she kicked and bawled, tossing her head back and forth, drenching

Mitchell with brown-black blood. Greg buckled under her incredible weight, finally lowering the blade, where her engorged carcass slid off and toppled to the floor in a heap.

Panting heavily, he rose. Raylene joined him as they watched the woman die.

"I-I'm sorry, Mama." Raylene's lip trembled.

But Mama laughed, a wheezing gurgle, coughing up more blood. "Traitorous child—you'll both get what you got comin'."

The boards underfoot creaked as they bent upward, lit from beneath by some hellish blood-red light. Greg and Raylene took hold of one another, staggering about as Mama cackled all the louder. "Now you gone and done it, holy man! You done woke up the Old Man of the House—and he'll see to it that you'll never make it long enough to die in that cabin in the woods!"

Mama spat and burbled, then grew still, her mad leer frozen to her dead face.

The farmhouse rattled as the black blood of the hooved creatures began to slither along the upending boards, inching up the wall, pulled together by sticky strands into a cancerous growth in the rafters. From that pulsating tumor, a deep guttural laugh threatened to make Greg vomit.

"It's him!" Raylene screamed.

"Who?" Greg shouted over the thunderous bellow.

Raylene faced him, holy fear in her eyes. "Maelfix!"

The two pivoted, as a face began to emerge from the bubbling slime. Tears stung Greg's eyes, his mind on the verge of snapping.

At last, he gripped his sister by the wrist and rushed for the door. *"Run!"*

Chapter Twelve

HAVERSHAM ROSE SLOWLY. He had not been having a good day. Oh, it had started well enough. He had thwarted his rival and laid claim to the House of Shadows, as his Order called it, but then his rival's young protégé became a fly in the ointment and everything went south rather quickly. Near spent, Thorvald gathered his wits and mustered what little healing magics he could, feeling the fractured radius knit itself back together. It still hurt to beat hell, but it would hold up so long as he didn't task it too much.

The magician kept his eyes on both rival and demon. Connors was sharp, but this alluring creature, this temptress, was old before the Earth was formed. It slithered about the void, in service to the infernal long before the Rebellion and Fall. The light of Grace had never fallen upon her and her ilk. Still, the demon was but a servant, tethered to one hellish prince after another, and if there was one thing the Black Spire was adept at, it was dealing with matters of Court.

Haversham steeled himself. To survive this, he would need to untap and harness eldritch energies that would all but incinerate lesser men, but, if he could entice Connors to do so in his stead, then the danger would be mitigated, and he might kill two birds with a proverbial stone. Might being the operative word. Was the risk worth taking? When had it ever not been? Haversham had risen within the ranks of the Spire by bold, calculated risks, by brokering deals with unseemly preternatural intelligences, and he had achieved almost all of his ambitions. Yet still, Connors and his Sacred Hart had always been there, keeping his ultimate goals at bay. Now his rival's Order was in shambles, all but finished. Where the father had been a seemingly steadying force in the battle between the forces of Light and Darkness, the son was reckless and prone to indecision. He lacked the father's instinct for cutting one's losses.

The magus pressed his palm against his chest, feeling the pulse of magical discourse radiating from the amulet he wore pressed against his flesh. It was a silver square and triangle, with three sapphires set in the points of a triangle that was within a gold ring. A lead bar bisected the three shapes. Haversham grimaced as the lead began to melt, the heat generated by his magic making short work of it and it alone. The bar was a lock, to keep the energies within the charm inert until called upon. The time to call upon those energies had come.

His eyes never left Connors' protective circle, even as the ceiling overhead thundered with a cacophony of screams and unholy rumblings from some unspeakable horror unleashed above. The true master of this little game had come home to roost, and Haversham was dead-set on coming out on the right side of this equation. The bar now gone, Haversham felt a swell of numinous calefaction pass over him. His vision blurred, and he found it near impossible to swallow. Rising slowly, he stepped outside of his shattered circle and approached that wrought by Connors. Bringing his hands to his chest, first in a symbol of mock prayer, the mage spread his palms wide, forming a triangle with his thumbs and forefingers. He pressed forward, extending his arms, feeling the protective circle give way. Haversham stepped through like a dragonfly swimming through molten amber, until he was within its magical confines and it reformed into a majestic sphere of defensive energy.

Connors snapped about. A look passed between them. Haversham saw a faint glimmer of fear take root in the other man, and for a moment the two were connected. The Englishmen was drawn into the young detective's mind, and he realized that the fear he'd sensed was not an emotion so much as a living, breathing, and sentient thing... a thing that lived in the icy imagination of a young man nearly broken by an impenetrable darkness that was the near personification of the great void itself. Somewhere, overhead, Maelfix raged and the House of Shadows trembled, but Thorvald Haversham took no notice, for he was no longer within its reality; he had become one with another, altogether different one. One that had been, but was ever-present, in the mind of Landon Connors. For a brief instant, Haversham saw the shade of the sultry demon that licked its lips in anticipation of feeding on both of their souls, or perhaps delivering them to her betters. She smiled at him as he descended into a frozen wasteland, a cavernous icy nightmare beyond all imagining.

He was Haversham no more. The Englishman was staring out through the eyes of a younger Landon Connors. Wrapped within layers of extreme weather clothing, Haversham found himself rappelling into an arctic grotto. The cold was unfathomable. Lantern light illuminated the stark cavern, everything cast in an incandescent blue refulgence. The lantern was at the feet of a man submerged in a bulky parka. Frosted goggles clung to his face, and below that, a tight wrap with nostril holes protected the flesh there. Haversham moved toward the figure, dropping the rappel line and adjusting the pack on his shoulders. The man nodded and lowered his face wrap to speak. It was Ashton Connors, young Landon's father, patriarch of the Connors clan, Ippissimus of the Sacred Hart, and, most assuredly, among the deceased.

"Are you alright?" the senior Connors asked. His eyes were cold, calculating, but there was a sense of urgency in his voice. It was then that Haversham realized that Landon's heartbeat was elevated, his breath short and labored. This was a lad in the grips of mind-numbing fear.

"Y-Yes," Landon said. "I'm fine."

"Good," Ashton said calmly. "If we're going to get out of here, I need you present. Do not succumb to fear. Use it. Manipulate it. Emotion can be a powerful fuel source if we do not let it overwhelm us."

"B-But, that *thing*, it..." Landon stammered. Ashton cut the boy down with an icy stare.

"That *thing* is a spawn of Kassogtha, boy, and if you want either of us to get out of this maze alive you'll get a hold of yourself and..."

Haversham saw something pass over the elder Connors' face in that moment. Ashton pushed his son aside, raising his hands as halos of ancient energies ignited there. From within Landon, Haversham looked back to see great black tendrils, tenebrous ink dripping from the appendages, reach out from the cavernous maw from which the two Connors had come.

The Englishman was stunned, as was his host. This malefic nightmare made flesh was a chthonic horror, wholly unnatural and perverse. Haversham was both repulsed and in awe. Its raw power was undeniable, but this was no mere beast. No, Haversham could sense its alien intellect, feel it probing into the recesses of his mind. There were no human words to describe what transpired there in mere seconds, the depth of knowledge that passed between them as visions of deep, impenetrable space, beyond the rim of this galaxy, into the far-flung reaches of a universe unfathomable, where creatures sailed on interstellar winds by magics that were used to form something out of nothing...

Haversham clung to his sanity by but the meagerest of threads, as did Landon Connors, as well. The boy had scrambled to his knees, casting ineffective spells in his father's defense. Ashton Connors was in the beast's oily grip, his magic little more than a nuisance. It all was unfolding in slow motion. Haversham desperately wanted to know what had led to this event, but captivated by the moment, it was the actions of this young man that took center stage.

As the oozing, dripping tentacles reached out for him, Landon Connors desperately inscribed a circle, roughly nine feet in diameter, in the cavern floor with his Grivel Ice Axe, and then with the spike end gouged out ancient sigils. From where the lad had culled this knowledge, Haversham could not fathom, but he recognized the power being tapped into, and it came in a flourish, building in intensity. Landon leapt to his feet, wielding the adze blade as a weapon, biting into the unnatural thing's flesh. He ran then, as fast as his legs would carry him, until a resounding cacophony erupted, an explosive magical discharge that brought the cavern down around them, the ceiling collapsing, forcing the unholy terror to retreat back from whence it came, leaving Landon Connors trapped beneath the crushing weight of ice and stone, his leg all but ruined by the esoteric carnage. And while he lived, it was the lifeless form of Ashton Connors being drug away into the black depths of the arctic grotto that was young Landon's last sight before unconsciousness consumed him.

It was then that Haversham was thrust back into his body. Standing behind Connors now, he realized now what horrors this lad had born witness to and what powers he had commanded in order to live. They were not so different after all, Haversham mused. No, not so different at all. And now, the raging fury of Maelfix above made sense, all too well. A pact had been entered into, one Connors at some point had weaseled out of, and this was all recompense. Haversham, resolved, spun Connors about and smiled.

"No," Connors whispered, but it was too late. As their eyes locked, the power was transferred, and Connors cried out in agony. Magical energy coursed through his body, his muscles grew taut and enflamed, and he was lifted up off the ground, lightning seemingly dancing from his fingertips as his eyes rolled back in his head. Spinning about, he waved his hand and the circle of protection was cast aside.

"Run, demon," he seethed, and the ancient thing cowered back, retreating from which it came.

It was then that Connor's protégé staggered down the stairs, the beautiful Miss Buckland in tow. They were both battered and bloody and running as if their lives depended on it. This proved to be quite accurate. Haversham backed into the corner as an explosion rocked the house, splintered wood raining down from above, a great hand descending and swatting the holy man and his charge as they were flung across the room. Maelfix descended.

"Connors," it hissed. "You are in my house now."

"In the name of Rael, Scourge of Demons, I command you—Be gone!"

A great cyclone of wind tore through the first floor, flinging furniture and raising debris. In the midst of this, Connors defied gravity, filled with the necromantic energies of the Black Spire's machination. The house crumbled beneath the weight of the magical conflagration, the walls exploding outward. Haversham shielded his eyes against the onslaught, barely able to see the battle that ensued. When the storm passed, Connors lay upon the ruined floor, the sky overhead a churning kaleidoscope of dark hues. Maelfix stood over the occult detective, triumphant, but a shell of its former self.

"So very close, little mage," Maelfix growled. The demon staggered forward and lifted Connors up from the wreckage. "Now, what to do with you?" The demon laughed, deep and guttural. With a wave of his hand, the house began to knit itself back together, reforming around them as if nothing had transpired.

Haversham stole across the room, carefully avoiding the demon's gaze. He helped Raylene to her feet, then offered his hand to Greg Mitchell. Mitchell rose gingerly. He was almost as wrecked as the house had been.

"The demon is at its weakest, boy," Haversham said. "We'll not have a better chance." He pulled out his last defense, a wax talisman upon which the Tetragrammaton was inscribed. "Shall we bring heaven and hell together and end this?"

"Abso-*freaking*-lutely," Mitchell replied.

Chapter Thirteen

LANDON CONNORS SQUIRMED IN the brimstone grip of the heathen god Maelfix. The giant's fingers closed about his chest, and the occult detective heard his ribs grating against each other. He gnashed his teeth in torment, sweating plentifully as he tried to search his extensive psychic library for the incantation to bring relief—but under such strain, his mind was void of all but indescribable pain. Connors was only diffusely conscious that the Hallowe'en House around him was rebuilding, board by board, in a storm of motion. Down below, shapes skittered back and forth across the floor, among them the hooved, shadowed things that had come to the house's aid. But also he glimpsed that snake Haversham, as well as his friend Mitchell and the alluring Raylene Buckland. The trio were shouting to one another, as Greg and Haversham traded demonic targets.

The two men, each positioned on polar opposite ends of the spiritual divide, stood back to back, brothers bathed in the blood of battle. Mitchell had his silver short sword out, crudely hacking and slashing, while the scheming Brit drew mystic symbols in the air with crooked fingers that burned bright orange before shooting out towards their targets. The cloudy apparitions snared in the corporeal incantations sizzled and screamed, exploding with pops of dark ichor gore.

"Hang on, Landon!" Mitchell cried, removing the head of an approaching ghoul with the polished edge of his blade.

"Yes, do hurry," Landon strained through clenched teeth.

All the while, Maelfix laughed, rattling the farmhouse even as it stitched itself back together. "You've eluded me too long, little wizard. Your payment is due. We have prepared such exquisite agonies for you in the Pit!"

The devil's fingers curled tighter, compacting Connors to the point of squeezing a scream from his throat. Just as suddenly, the infernal digits loosened, followed by the distinct bark of a .357 Ruger. Landon dipped his head to the side and saw Mitchell there, panting heavily, his sword resting on its blood-soaked tip, his recently-fired revolver in his other hand aimed right at Maelfix.

"Hey!" the foolhardy Outrider hailed. "Got your attention yet?"

Maelfix's eyes closed to scrutinizing slits. "You think even your iron bullets would have any effect on me, slave of God? I would have thought Connors taught you better than that, boy."

Mitchell smirked, defiant. "He did. First rule in a wizard's book—*distraction*."

From the opposite direction, a thunderclap slammed against Maelfix and his captive like a wall, and Connors swiveled to see Haversham at the top of the stairs, weaving an impossibly complex Solomon's Key. The older man was slumped and perspiring, his tie and collar loosened, his sleeves scrunched up to his elbows, utilizing whatever reserves he kept hidden for self-preservation, exhausting every last ounce of his will. As a result, the Key burned molten, materializing to form a rippling pattern of psychokinetic energy.

Semi-translucent horned figures of murderous intent clambered up the stairs, groping along the walls and railing, clawing for him. Haversham ignored them, muttering feverishly his prayer—to what god, Connors didn't dare ask. He was simply thankful for the assist, from *wherever* the help originated.

Still, the phantasms neared the Brit, screaming in rage, their vaporous tendrils sharpening to long spears. Haversham seemed at his bloody end, even as Maelfix's grip gradually faded to immateriality. *Just a moment more, old boy*, Connors thought, urging on the Englishman, *and I'll be free.* It seemed, though, that Haversham hadn't a moment more—until the seductive Raylene Buckland charged the stairs, reciting a verse in an unknown tongue that set Connors' soul to wilting.

Starting in the back of her throat, a burbling mass of ghostly blue-white ectoplasm surfaced, then unfurled like an octopus. Its tendrils exploded with motion, lancing through the spectral invaders, piercing their hazy shapes. The beasts screeched and writhed, as the oozing mass crawled over them, reeling them in—all the way back into Raylene. She dropped to her knees, black trickling from her eyes, as she slowly devoured the shapes, consuming them until the staircase was cleansed. Once through, she released a hellish scream, then dropped to all fours, coughing and wheezing.

It was only then that Connors realized her incredible display had captivated the entire room, as even Maelfix stared upon the girl, stupefied. Only Haversham did not lose himself in her exhibition, but chose the hard-won respite to finish his arduous work.

At last, Maelfix's body turned to soupy fog, and Connors easily slipped past, covering himself with brown-black gunk as he passed through what once had been the devil's arm and hand. The detective landed hard on the floor, and Mitchell was there a heartbeat later, all smiles.

"Are you alright?" he shouted in excitement as, behind him, a geyser of tar—the very essence of the dread Maelfix—fought to reform while the house boards shifted and sorted uncertainly, allowing shafts of rainbow-coloured lights to spill into the sifting foyer. The gelatinous tower churned with intelligence, then sighted Mitchell and punched forward for the hunter.

"Behind you!" Connors shouted, fumbling in his coat for a ward or talisman. Beating him to the task, Mitchell spun, shielding the detective with his body, and held out a commanding hand, his fingers splayed.

"No, demon! Here, and no further! The God of Heaven adjures thee!"

A flickering dome of holy energy fizzled and danced around their periphery, and the pillar of gunk splashed against it, its strength spent. Mitchell lowered his hand, removing the barrier, then gripped Connors by the elbow and heaved. "Come on, 'old man'," he grinned, and Connors did likewise, regaining his balance.

Away from the action, Landon spied Baltruska, the portal to her eternal library beckoning at her back. She seemed to sense the unraveling of the situation, surveying the scene with apprehension. As she met Connors' gaze, she adjusted her anxiety and grinned almost seductively. "Looks like we will have to postpone our little engagement, sweets," she said, then faded into her library realm, the doorway closing and fading from view.

Connors was thankful that they had one less villain to contend with. All about them, the house continued to shuffle in confusion, as Maelfix's essence stirred in the rafters, trying to regather its shape and strength. Mitchell braced himself on the banister and hollered, "Haversham! We're leaving!"

The Englishman nodded, fatigued, carefully descending the steps, using the railing for support, while the house buckled and its Master bellowed. Connors watched his rival, but a sharp cry stole his attention. He glanced to the floor, where young Raylene continued to fight against the hellspawn she'd ingested. With every wince, every cough, the house shuddered.

He rubbed at his beard worriedly. "Hm."

Mitchell was there at the foot of the stairs, lending a helping hand to Haversham, assisting the older man in a hobble. "We gotta get out of this house before it falls apart."

"Wait," Connors said, his tone calmer than he actually felt. "We're in the spaces between the worlds. If we leave now—"

"He's right," Haversham panted in Mitchell's grip. "We'll be lost to time and space, adrift as little more than stardust."

Connors knew as much, but had already pieced together their answer. Raylene squirmed in pain, and the house responded in kind. Gradually, the implications dawned on his peers as well.

"She's a psychopomp," Greg said with something like awe, or maybe horror. "Just like 'Mama'. She controls this house. Mama wanted *me* to—"

In a fit of panic, Connors gripped Mitchell by the jacket. "What did you say to her? Did you *agree?*"

Greg's lip curled in surprise and revulsion. "Of course not! Are you nuts? I told her 'no' and shoved a sword through her gut just in case I wasn't clear enough."

Connors' grip relinquished, and he hung his head. "Good. Very good."

"Landon, what's—"

Raylene clutched her belly, pregnant with a thousand unspeakable evils, and screamed. Mitchell left Haversham to wobble on his own, then raced to the frail creature. He knelt down before her, taking her by the shoulders, surprising Landon with his tenderness. What had transpired in that upper room? What bond had formed between them that the girl would turn against her mother and, indeed, the Master of this accursed farmhouse?

"Stay with me," Mitchell implored her. "You're going to be okay. We're going to get out of here. My friends can help you. We'll start over."

She nodded in a hurry, whimpering as she bit down on her lip, and he smiled kindly upon her, touching her damp cheek. Connors allowed himself the briefest moment of admiration for the moving scene, but the cancer in the rafters was growing thicker, pulsating with wickedness, and the face of Maelfix returned.

"Connors!" it croaked, and Landon knew what had to be done.

"I'm sorry, Greg," he muttered.

"What are you—?"

Then Landon Connors drew the athame from his inside coat pocket and slid it into Raylene's back. She gasped, her eyes staring straight ahead in fear before eventually rolling into the back of her head, and Mitchell desperately fumbled to catch her. The woman slumped forward into his waiting arms, and the young man gaped at Connors in abject shock and rage. "What did you do? My God, Landon, *what did you do?*"

The growing evil overhead squealed, and the farmhouse came apart in a violent storm, loose boards swirling in the air with abandon. Haversham cursed and took cover. Connors narrowly avoided a projectile, himself, but Mitchell was focused intently on him, cradling the dead woman. The wizard opened his mouth to apologize—and only saw the plank hurtling towards him at the last minute.

Next, he saw black.

LANDON CONNORS AWOKE, and his face met with crisp, autumn evening air. He sat up with a sharp inhale and glanced around at the empty field in Alix, Arkansas. The farmhouse was gone, not even its foundation remaining. Insects resumed their nighttime chorus, rejoicing that the nightmare was finally over. Only the stars illuminated his vision, but a black blob startled him overhead. He flinched, until a liver-spotted hand emerged, and a familiar voice echoed, "Well done, mate."

Connors met Haversham's gloating face. The man looked better, like he'd caught his breath, but he was still disheveled from their ordeal. Reluctantly, Landon accepted the aid and rose, minding his bum knee. He searched the grounds for his cane, thankful to find it some feet away. He limped for it while Haversham watched.

"A fair spot of deduction, old boy. Reasoning that poor Miss Buckland was the tether keeping Maelfix to the physical plane. You do realize, however, that he's not dead. I imagine he's scattered to the cosmic winds, but, in time, he'll reconstitute. You've only bought yourself time."

Connors groaned as he retrieved his cane from the grass. "That'll have to do for now."

Haversham straightened with some effort and faced the blasted patch of earth where the house once stood. "A shame about the House of Shadows, though. The knowledge we could've gained—"

Connors snorted in derision. "Knowledge. Please. You only came here for power."

Haversham smirked, then added a wink. "And now that's gone, too. Not many mysteries left in this world, mate. Not to our ilk, at any rate. One fewer now. Will you miss it?"

Landon considered the truth of that statement. All the secrets of the spheres they could have gleaned from a house that traveled the timelines. He shared in Haversham's reflective silence, mourning the loss in his own way, then saw Greg Mitchell some distance away, knelt on the ground, the still form of Raylene Buckland on his lap. He firmed his jaw and showed his tense profile to his rival. "Now's your chance to leave, Thorvald. While I'm too tired to kill you like I should."

The Briton smirked. "Until next time, chap."

A sudden gust of wind stirred Connor's hair, and when he turned, the wicked man was gone. *And good riddance.*

Braced on his cane, Landon traversed the empty field, arriving at his friend's side. "It was the only way," he offered quietly.

Greg did not face him. "I know."

"Do not think that made the deed any easier."

Mitchell sniffed, carefully laid Raylene aside, then stood rigid. Still facing her, he said, "I've got shovels in the back of the truck. Help me bury her?"

"Aye, lad. I will."

The two men set to it, working in silence as Hallowe'en passed into cool November morning.

Epilogues

THE DRIVE BACK TO INDIANA had been quiet and tense. Greg told Landon what had transpired in the farmhouse's upper chambers, but only in vague terms, omitting the truth of Raylene's heritage and her connection to him. Why he spared the detective those details, Greg didn't know. Out of shame, or perhaps to ease Connors' already overburdened conscience? It was of little consequence now. The matter was concluded, and neither man had reason to speak of it again.

Greg hadn't offered any sort of good-bye at the end of their long drive, merely pulling up to Caliburn House, letting off his murderous passenger without comment, then heading for the last leg of this journey—the one he had to traverse alone.

Once more, he found himself in the hospital hallway, aimed for his father's room. This time, he sensed no tingling sensation of *other* eyes, no outside forces prying into his affairs. Perhaps Maelfix's recent disintegration had left a vacancy in the kingdom of the air, and the devils were crowded together in some forgotten hall of hell to mourn the defeat of one of their dukes. That was all for the best if it were true, for Greg had yet to rebuild his mental or emotional defenses. He operated on little sleep, and the road had worn him down. His spirit was laid bare, easy prey for any unseen predator. Now that the adrenaline of the fight was finally subsiding, the doubts and fears that Mama Buckland had implanted to use against him back at the House of Shadows flooded his mind without restraint. All he could think about was that damnable cabin in the woods and the premonition of Landon standing over him, removing his head…

A day ago, he'd never have believed his friend capable of such cold-hearted butchery. But this had been an eventful Hallowe'en in that regard, and Greg had yet to entirely wash Raylene's dried blood from his clothes.

He rounded the corner to his father's room and saw what he'd feared. Kat was there, comforting their mother, as both women wept openly. His nephew and niece were there, too, sobbing softly where they sat.

Greg's shoulders sagged, his stomach cringing, and his throat went dry.

Kat looked up over Mom's shoulder and saw him. Her wet face shriveled in indignant rage, and she left the trembling woman to storm in his direction. "Get out!"

Greg ignored her outburst. "When did it happen?"

"Where were you? We called and we *called* you."

He couldn't ignore the irony, since she'd been the one to call the cops on him the first time he attempted to visit the dying man. "I had something I had to take care of."

"Well I hope it was important," she spat. She looked him up and down in disgust. "I'd *slap* you if I thought you actually cared enough to show up and not just send your damned *ghost!*"

"Kat—"

"Leave us alone," she huffed, then returned to her family—to his family. She collected her children and his mother, loving and protective towards everyone but him, and escorted them away, but not before fixing him with a withering curse of a glare.

Greg hung back, then turned about to his father's doorway. He entered, interrupting nurses as they unhooked the machines that had kept Bro. Bill alive in his final days. They'd already draped the sheet over his father's lifeless face, and their own visages turned as white as corpses as Greg entered.

"Can I have a moment alone with my dad?" he managed, his voice weak and strange-sounding to his own ears.

He recognized a couple of the staff from his earlier visit—and they remembered him, too. They backed away from him in a fright, careful not to touch his manifestation, and bumbled into equipment to vacate the room. He waited for them to leave, wondering if they were on their way to find security. Not that it would matter. He'd be far away from this place before they arrived. His business here wouldn't take long.

Steeling his resolve, he stepped up to the body beneath the blanket.

Then his very physical hand took hold of the blanket and removed it.

Greg recoiled in despair, for his father's face was not peaceful as he'd supposed, but twisted in fright and pain.

He'll die screaming in the dark, boy, Mama Buckland had said, *and no one will be there with him in the final hour.*

At last, Greg broke down, throwing himself across his father's scrawny, still chest, and sobbed. When he could find the words again, he whispered, "It's done, Dad. The witch is dead."

He rose, wiping at his eyes and face and nose, and this time, as he looked on his father's countenance, Bill Mitchell's muscles seemed to relax, his mouth resuming a natural shape, and he looked at rest. In that moment, Greg noted the shape of his father's eyes and recognized Raylene in them.

The Outrider smiled through tears, returned the sheet to preserve the man's dignity, and left the hospital behind, stepping out into the light of a new day.

THORVALD HAVERSHAM STEPPED OUT of the hackney on the corner of Hazlitt and Blythe and raised the collar of his black trench coat against the chill wind blowing out of Shepherd's Bush. A steady drizzle fell out of the grey sky, but the street was still littered with the inebriated and dispossessed. A young couple, Americans, he surmised, staggered toward him. The woman, a pretty bottled blonde, reached for Haversham's arm and asked, "Pardon me, sir, do you know the way to Holland Park?"

"At this hour?" Haversham scoffed.

"The sun'll be up soon," her companion replied. "We were told we could grab a wink there without hassle from the cops."

"No, that won't do," Haversham said warmly. He lifted the young woman's chin ever so slightly. She reminded him of someone, someone he'd cared for years before, before his path veered left of center and the Spire wrapped its tentacles about him in a tenebrous embrace. He shuddered as he added, "I've a room here, at number 36." He removed a key from his inner pocket, a skeleton key with an elaborately flourished bow and triangular bit. "Take it. Get some well-earned sleep. We'll break fast together come mid-morning and you will repay me by sharing your story."

"We couldn't," the young woman said.

"You can and you shall," Haversham said, pressing the key into her palm. "Now, along with you both. My ward will show you to bed and we shall become acquainted over bangers and black pudding."

They muttered drunken thank yous and staggered off toward Haversham's let while he set himself back to course. He knew *they* would be waiting for him, the Secret Chiefs, and a full report would be expected. His failure would, of course, not go unpunished, but he was confident that the information gleaned from the debacle would temper their hand. Somewhat. A cock crowed as he spotted the vintage lorry, a burgundy and mustard yellow transport, idling in front of the Beaconsfield. Emblazoned on the panel were the words BLACK MOUNTAIN SIDESHOW, CARNIVAL, AND REVUE. He paused to meditate on the corporate sigil, a crescent moon above a radiant sun with three triangles within.

The driver stepped out and walked to the back of the van, knocked three times, then raised the door. The interior was heavily shadowed, sparse candlelight caressing the dark. Aged tapestries were hung over the sidewalls and ceiling. Haversham climbed inside and the driver closed the door behind him.

"Sit," a dark figure said, motioning with an arm toward the unoccupied Welsh Wingback. They were three in number. Two women and a man. The man was still and silent, sitting between the two women. It was the woman to his left that had spoken, while the one to his right whispered into the man's ear. Haversham took his seat.

The woman on the left said, "You have passed through the Trial of Fire."

"I have, your grace," Haversham replied, head bowed.

"The excellence of result has reference to perfection and imperfection," the woman on the right said. A flicker of the candle's flame altered her countenance, shifting from the rosy glow of transcendent beauty to feral beast by the trick of the light. "The mature being more perfect than the immature," she continued. "Now, maturity is altogether due to the heat of fire. Hence fire holds the highest place among active elements."

"And the boy?" the man asked from the shadows.

"Connors?" Haversham said, swallowing hard.

"Yes," the woman on the left hissed.

"He took the magic's full measure," Haversham replied. "It was harrowing, to be sure, but I played my part."

"Yet lost the Shadow House," the woman on the right said. Her tone was cold.

"Unfortunate," Haversham said as calmly as he could muster, "but unavoidable. Maelfix is a formidable foe."

"And still on the board," the woman responded quickly. She leaned forward and whispered to the woman to the left, who stood and stepped more fully into the light, her naked flesh accentuated by the candle's flame.

"I am the keeper of the shadow," she said. She licked her fingertips and snuffed out a candle. Holding out her hand, the other woman took it and rose, stepping into the scant light, her naked body covered in arcane runes.

"I am the keeper of the night," she said as she snuffed out the candle before her. The two women walked toward the back of the transport, lost in the swallowing darkness. A single candle still cast a meek light. Its flame danced as the man leaned forward, the light dancing across his face.

"Connors," the man said. "He has grown?"

"He is a true adept, Magus," Haversham replied. "Few have his talent and raw ability, but he is challenged. I sense a tremendous weight upon him."

"And Mitchell?"

"Devout," Haversham said. "He is a man of faith, but saddled with self-doubt and guilt." He paused, reflecting on their brief alliance. "There is a wedge between teacher and student." Haversham shifted uneasily. "Their relationship is not unlike a father and son."

The man leaned forward even more, further into the light, his features gaunt and chiseled, a spider-web of scars along the left side of his face. "One does not truly become a man until the death of the father," he said. He held his palm above the flame, allowing it to lick at him until the smell of burnt flesh filled the lorry interior.

"Magus?"

"I don't feel the flame," he said. "Not anymore." His eyes turned black then, and he smiled. Ashton Connors laughed, low and hushed. "If their relationship mirrors that of father and son, one wonders, if a man is made so by a father's death, then what when a son dies?"

"By your command," Haversham said, head bowed.

"Make it so."

Afterword

THE DEAD WILL NOT GO QUIET

Nearly a decade ago now, I was asked by a friend to submit a story to *Coach's Midnight Diner*, a "faith-based" anthology of hard-boiled horror, mystery, and paranormal fiction. While I wasn't a Christian, I often wrote horror fiction that used themes culled from Judeo-Christian Cosmology. I tossed around a few ideas, ultimately settling on an excerpt from the novel I was working on at the time, *Descendant*. The excerpt concerned a priest who was an occult detective, of sorts. It had some real punch. I liked it a lot and it was, ultimately, well-received.

When *Midnight Diner: The Back from the Dead Edition* came out I was less than thrilled with the overall quality of the stories I found "Queen's Gambit" sharing a table of contents with. One story, though, stood out to me. It was called "Flowers for Shelly" and it was written by a young man from Arkansas named Greg Mitchell. "Flowers for Shelly" had heart. It was obviously somewhat biographical —*the best stories usually are*—and I thought the author had real promise.

As fate would have it, Greg kind of dug "Queen's Gambit" too. He reached out through social media and we began corresponding, quickly finding that, despite our religious differences, we had a lot in common— we were both 'family men' with deep Arkansas roots and were fairly obsessed with horror and pop culture. We bonded quickly, discussed writing frequently, and when I was tapped to write a prequel story connected to my novel *Descendant*, I named a character after my newfound compatriot.

Greg Mitchell, the character, was an Outrider, one of several occult investigators that had been trained by my main protagonist, Dr. Landon Connors, in the esoteric arts. "The Cabin in the Woods", originally published by Ghostwriter Publications in late 2009, found Connors called to Wisconsin and the scene of a grisly death—enter Greg Mitchell: occult expert, exorcist, and freshly minted corpse.

The thing is, Greg Mitchell wouldn't stay dead. Well, that's not entirely accurate. More like, he wouldn't stay buried. Greg Mitchell, again, the character, was a part of the Liber Monstrorum Mythos, an important cog in the Landon Connors Universe.

The demonologist was oft mentioned, with little nods here and there and brief appearances in flashbacks and prequels, but then, in 2014, Mitchell showed up unexpectedly in a serialized story I wrote called "Wyrdtails". In it, we find that Mitchell is a ghost, tethered as a sort of moral compass to Connors as he becomes embroiled in a mystery involving old college roommates and an ancient grimoire.

If you were to ask me which of my short stories is my favorite, it's that one, and the character of Greg Mitchell is a big part of why that story worked so well for me.

Tick the clock forward a few years and you'll find us in 2017. Greg Mitchell, the author, reached out to me about collaborating on a Landon Connors story, a prequel involving Greg Mitchell, the character, in what ultimately became the tale you just finished. He fired off the basic premise and I did not hesitate to say "yes".

Greg had become a dear and trusted friend. When I had good news, I dropped him a line. When a publisher had me pulling my hair out, I dropped him a line. When I needed to chat with someone who understood the ups and downs of a writer's life, I dropped him a line. So when he said he wanted to take a stroll through the Liber Monstrorum, there was no way I was going to say "no".

I truly hope you enjoyed reading "Hallowe'en House" as much as we enjoyed spinning it. The collaboration was slow going at times. It was a rough haul for me personally as my father was battling cancer pretty much through the entire process. It was a battle he ultimately lost just a few months back.

"Hallowe'en House" was a refuge for me.

Even when I wasn't writing my chapters, I was thinking about them, and that respite, while I was helping to look after my ailing father, was a refuge I greatly needed. I think you'll find certain themes floating through the story that reflect the emotional strain and turmoil both Greg and myself were going through as "Hallowe'en House" was taking form.

Did it make for a better story?

Maybe.

We all channel pain in different ways and haul about our emotional baggage as best we can. We writers tend to bleed it out on the page. Not that "Hallowe'en House" is some sort of cathartic Hallmark moment. But it was what the doctor ordered.

Well, Dr. Connors, that is.

One thing's for sure, we've not seen the last of Greg Mitchell, the character.

When you're a ghost, it's kind of hard to get rid of you...

—Bob Freeman
writing from the
Lost Sister Trail
September 25, 2018

About the Authors

BOB FREEMAN is an author, artist, and paranormal adventurer whose previous novels include *Shadows Over Somerset*, *Keepers of the Dead*, and *First Born*. A lifelong student of mythology, folklore, magic, and religion, Freeman has written numerous short stories, articles, and reviews for various online and print publications and is a respected lecturer on the occult and paranormal phenomena. He lives in rural Indiana with his wife Kim and son Connor. Mr. Freeman can be found at: www.occultdetective.com.

GREG MITCHELL is a screenwriter and novelist and author of *The Coming Evil Trilogy*. His eclectic career includes eight novels, several short stories, a small contribution to the *Star Wars Expanded Universe*, and two Syfy Channel Original Movies—*Snakehead Swamp* and *Zombie Shark*. He lives in Northeast Arkansas with his wife and two daughters. Visit him online at: www.thecomingevil.blogspot.com.

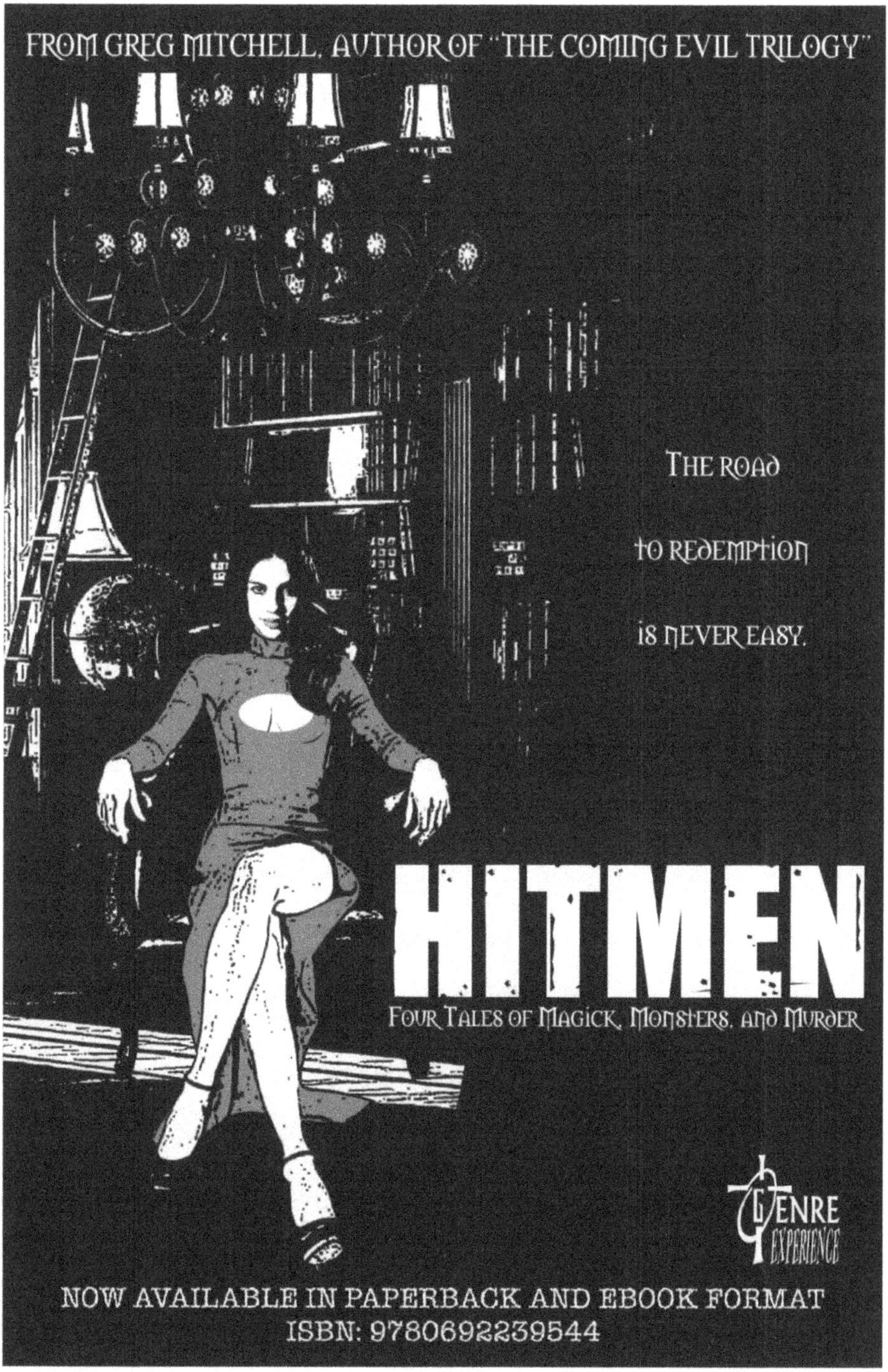
FROM GREG MITCHELL, AUTHOR OF "THE COMING EVIL TRILOGY"
THE ROAD
TO REDEMPTION
IS NEVER EASY.
HITMEN
FOUR TALES OF MAGICK, MONSTERS, AND MURDER
GENRE EXPERIENCE
NOW AVAILABLE IN PAPERBACK AND EBOOK FORMAT
ISBN: 9780692239544

Printed in the USA
CPSIA information can be obtained
at www.ICGtesting.com
LVHW041638291023
762496LV00026B/204